Hal Graff

Love and Death in the Dominican Republic

A Harold Gatewood Mystery

Volume 9

Hal Graff

D1785545

Love and Death in the Dominican Republic

For Eric, Lainen, Colton, Ethan, Jenny, Scott, Finn, and Kade

Hal Graff

Copyright 2017

ISBN: 13:978-1542850117
ISBN: 10:1542850118

Disclaimer

Love and Death in the Dominican Republic

Contents

Hal Graff

Prologue

THE WIND WHISTLED ACCROSS THE END ZONE of the Gibson City football field, past the baseball backstop, and kicked up dirt near home plate. Gatewood watched the swirls of dust blow across the infield and then escape into the outfield. He wished he could be like the dirt, as he also wanted to be swept away to a better, more peaceful place.

Harold sat near home plate holding Luisa in his arms. He looked down at her lifeless body and wondered why she had to die. All she had done was love him, and now she was dead, the same as all of the women he had loved.

Lore Lehoi had been forced by the AIO to choose between her parents or Gatewood. She had chosen her parents and was shot and killed by San Toro de Lidia, Spain lead detective Estebe Jakome when she was trying to kill Gatewood. Her death had broken his heart but he had the resolve to recover and help bring down the AIO's leadership in Northern Spain.

Christina Abene, was killed at the Havana, Cuba airport by AIO assassin Bakar Kemen when Gatewood and she were on their way to America to start a new life together. She had died in his arms, using her last words to tell Harold that she loved him.

His wife, Akemi Gang Gatewood, and their unborn son Tai, were killed by Yakaza crime family head

Love and Death in the Dominican Republic
Masaru Hayato on a distant riverbank in Inner Mongolia while fishing for taimen. Harold remembered his terrified thoughts in that awful moment he had seen Hayato slit Akemi's throat and stab her three times in her abdomen, killing Tai in the womb. He remembered choking Hayato over and over, and killing him.

He had then thrown the man's lifeless body to the ground, where it landed in the river, and stayed next to the bank. Harold remembered the river current taking control of the corpse, moving it into the main channel, and downstream. Soon, the body had moved into the current, down the center of the river, and around the bend, never to be seen again. It would become protein for the bears, or the wolves that lived in that region of the country.

Harold had not felt guilt, shame, or disgust for what he had done. He had avenged Akemi and Tai's deaths, and he had made sure that the man, Yakuza Yamaguchi Gumi crime lord Masaru Hayato, would not terrorize anyone else ever again. Harold knew that at that moment his life had changed forever. He had lost much of his life's joy, and had started to become hardened by the horrific act, and his loss of two more people he loved.

Yeong Hyeon, the beautiful North Korean spy and wonderful woman he loved, also met her death as they were planning on spending their lives together. She had lost her life when she was trying to save Harold's. She had been jerked overboard and eaten by a massive tiger shark as she attempted to help Harold on to the boat during their scuba diving outing in Islamorada, Florida.

Now, Luisa was dead, shot by Susana Richards, the deranged woman from Scalp, Minnesota, in a cruel act of torture and murder. Susana was a dangerous psychopath who had also murdered three other victims who had treated Gatewood unfairly. She was dangerous, and while he did not fear for his own life, he was worried about his parents and other loved ones who might enter his life, and become her next victims. He would need to develop a plan to deal with Susana.

Each death haunted Gatewood. All of the women had died because they had loved him. All had given their hearts to him and it had cost them their lives. It wasn't fair. They had deserved better fates.

He held Luisa's body close to him and looked out at the baseball diamond where he had spent his formative baseball years. He wondered what events would now unfold in his life. He wanted the many nightmares to disappear but he did not know how to bring the horror to an end.

He was tired of hitmen who wanted his head as a trophy, the AIO, the Yakuza, the TCPLM, the espionage game, the killings, the deranged dictators, and the female stalkers. The stress of his life over the last few years had taken a toll on his body and mind. He felt alone, and devastated.

He was tired, very tired.

Love and Death in the Dominican Republic

Chapter 1

Patience

August 18

AS GATEWOOD SAT WITH HIS BACK AGAINST THE BASEBALL BACKSTOP, the rusty wire mesh of the screen cut into his back. The texture of wire mesh had always been the same, rusty and memorable. He glanced out across the baseball diamond and was flooded with memories.

He had enjoyed many wonderful moments with his teammates and had performed his many successes on the field in front of him. Now, with Luisa's dead body in his arms, and her dried blood, bone, and DNA splattered on his clothes, none of the memories seemed to matter. He tried not to look at the damage that Susana Richard's rifle cartridge had caused when it had ripped through Luisa's head. He had covered the back of her head with his handkerchief to hide the horror of the wound.

He sat quietly, not speaking or crying, and gathered his thoughts. He would miss Luisa as they had a deep love for each other. They had been through many harrowing events together. She had enriched his life through her presence. He also thought about how he would settle the score with Susana Richards. He was

Hal Graff

not a vindictive man, but in this case he would make an exception to that rule.

His gaze was fixed on second base, where he had thrown out so many runners trying to steal, when he focused on a figure of a man walking toward him. He did not know who the man was, but as the distance between them grew shorter he saw the familiar face of policeman David Springer.

Springer covered the remaining distance, stopped, kneeled won on his right knee and said, "Harold, this is patrolman David Springer. Are you alright ?"

Gatewood replied, "Yes."

"Is Luisa alive."

"No."

"What happened ?"

"She killed her."

"Who killed her ?"

"Susana Richards.'

"Can you tell me what happened ?"

"She told me to go to the high school and park in the lot behind the boy's locker room. Then, I was ordered to walk across the street, and enter the baseball diamond. I was ordered to walk in from the outfield and stop at home plate. I was to remain there until I heard from Susana. She told me not to leave the home plate area."

"Very good Harold. Then what happened ?"

"I did as I was instructed. I stood at home plate and looked in horror at the backstop. Luisa was tied to the wire screen. Her arms were outstretched and her legs were bound together. She was tied in a manner of a person being crucified on a cross. Her head was hanging down, her chin on her chest. I called her name and she raised her head, and looked at me, her eyes begging for help. She had been beaten. Blood had dried on her face, near her nostrils."

"Go on Harold."

"My cell phone rang. I answered. It was Susana Richards. She told me that Luisa was tied to the backstop, in all of her glory. She said that she and Luisa had had a nice conversation about me. She said that, eventually, Luisa had agreed to be here, like this, waiting for me."

"What did you do then ?"

"I looked around to see if I could see Susana Richards. I scanned the bleachers, the area behind the backstop, the track, and the weight room area behind the baseball dugouts. She was not there. I wanted to go to Luisa but did not dare to do so as I had been warned to stay put."

"Go on."

"Susana then asked if I liked how Luisa looked. I told her she was very cruel to say that. She said that perhaps she was but that she did it to get my attention. I told her that she had to let Luisa go. She refused, and said that Luisa had to pay for making me run all over Mexico to find her. I then asked if I could go to the fence to talk with Luisa. She said that she wanted me to do that."

"Did you do it ?"

Hal Graff

"Yes.

"What did you say ?"

"First, I hugged her. Then I told her everything would be okay."

"What happened then ?"

"Susana made fun of me, saying that my actions were very touching, but that things were not going to be okay. She then ordered me to kiss Luisa."

"Did you ?"

"Yes, I did what I was ordered to do as I thought I could still find a way to save Luisa. I kissed her, wiped the blood from her nose, and then told her I was going to free her from the situation she was in at the time."

"Go on."

"Susana then told me to hold her."

"Did you ?"

"Yes, I quickly untied the ropes that bound Luisa to the backstop and held her in my arms. She meekly kissed me, as she was exhausted physically. I meekly returned the kiss and told her things were going to be alright."

"What happened next Harold ?"

"Susana told me to kiss her again. I did and told her that I loved her. Susana then told me that kiss was my goodbye kiss to Luisa."

"What did you do ?"

"I did not know what to do. Then I heard a shot. The bullet from Susana's rifle raced through the air, entered Luisa's head, and splattered blood, bone, and brain tissue on my face, arms, and hands. Luisa's body went limp, and both of us slumped to the ground. I held her lifeless body to my chest and then I started to sob."

"I understand Harold."

"We had made a long journey together, through many harrowing events in Venezuela, and then meeting again in Mexico."

"You were very close."

"Yes. David, it was not right that Luisa and my future together would end like this, her dead in my arms, both of us sitting on the ground by the backstop."

"I know Harold. What happened then ?"

"I heard a car engine start, looked at the far end of the football field, and saw a car speed away on to Sangamon Street, and head North out of town. Susana then called me and said that she would be seeing me soon."

"How are you feeling ?"

"Obviously, I am shaken. But I am not stirred to the point where I can't do what is needed."

"What kind of car was it ?"

"It was a white one. It was a small one, maybe a compact model. Like the ones you would get when you rent a car. I am not a car guy so I can't really tell one model from another."

"Where is Susana from Harold ?"

"Scalp, Minnesota. But, I don't think she will go back there. She is too smart for that. She probably has planned out her next moves very precisely and will be hard to find."

Hal Graff

"We will alert the state police. Alden Zorn is a great trooper and lives here in town and will help get an all-points bulletin out on her.

"Thanks. But she won't be found. She is way too smart, and devious, to be captured so easily."

"I have called the funeral home. I will stay here and I process the murder scene. Are you alright to accompany the hearse with Luisa's body to the funeral home ?"

"Yes, I will follow them in my car."

"Is there anything else I can do for you Harold ?"

"I am going to call my parents and tell them what happened, and that I am going to the funeral home. Can you please send another patrolman to my parents' home and have him stay there until I get there ? I am going to stay with them tonight. I don't think Susana Richards would do anything to my parents tonight but I want to make sure."

"I will."

After the funeral home people arrived and loaded Luisa's body into the hearse, Harold followed them to the funeral home, made arrangements to have Luisa buried next to him in his family's plot, and said he would take care of the funeral expenses. He then walked across the street and entered his boyhood church.

Harold walked through the doors of the church, went up the stairs, turned right, and walked to the row of pews in the center of the room. He sat down and silently said a prayer. Then, he looked around, and attempted to understand the many thoughts swirling around in his head.

He was sad, angry at Susana Richards for killing Luisa, and needed to wrestle with his beliefs and what he had planned to do with Susan Richards. He looked at the beautiful, tall, stained-glass windows at the right of the pulpit.

He had always loved them. He had spent many hours gazing at them, most of which were done at the expense of listening to the sermons. They had given him much enjoyment. He was now looking at them in a different state of mind, as he was torn between letting the authorities handle Susana Richards and doing what he knew he would have to do when their paths crossed again.

An unnoticed man approached him from his right, sat down next to him, and put his hand on his shoulder.

"Hello Harold."

It was his minister of many years, a man who had helped him greatly. He was a former baseball coach who had heard his calling and entered the ministry. He and Harold had worked together with the youth baseball program for many years when he was in high school and college. He was a man Harold greatly respected, and liked.

"Harold, I heard what happened and thought you might like to talk."

"Thank you."

"I know what a terrible tragedy this has been for you. On top of everything else you have endured over the last few years I know this is a heavy weight on your shoulders."

"Yes, it is."

"Remember, you are not alone in dealing with this situation. You have a strong faith and you will be guided through this hour of darkness."

"I know. Thank you for those kind thoughts. You have always given me great advice."

"You have always been a thoughtful listener and intelligent processor of information."

They talked about how he and Luisa had met, their path to closeness and love, events in Venezuela, their reunion in Mexico, and their plans they had made for the future. Harold was relieved when his minister agreed to do the graveside service at the cemetery. Harold then confessed his dilemma between following the commandments and doing what he feared he must do when Susana Richards would enter his life again.

He was relieved when his minister said that he should defend himself and do what was necessary to prevent being killed by an obviously deranged woman. He told Harold that killing a person in self-defense to save his life was alright, if one promised to use the rest of his life to do the right things as outlined by the scriptures. He urged Harold to let the authorities handle Susana Richards, but to be prepared to protect himself, just in case.

Harold thanked his minister, mentor, and friend for the good advice and then walked to his car to head to his parent's house for the night. He looked at the large side yard of church and smiled as he remembered how much he liked coming to church camp because there would be enough kids to play baseball during recess. He had been confirmed in his church and continued to be a member. It had never let him down.

Despite his minister's comforting words, Harold knew in his heart that the authorities would not be able to stop the inevitable confrontation between Susana and himself. He knew he must be ready to defend himself, and to kill her.

Chapter 2

Supply Lines

August 20

DIEGO RAMIREZ SAT IN THE OUTER OFFICE OF the TCPLM building looking at the empty desk that was formerly the workspace of Luisa Gaicia. He had come to power due to the death of Sergio Rojas. Rojas had been shot and killed by Harold Gatewood when the former head of the TCPLM refused to jump to his death from the top of the cable car in the mountains outside Caracas.

Ramirez had been with Rojas and the TCPLM since he joined the organization as a teenager. Rojas had invaded his village and rained havoc on the people due to his need to instill their total cooperation in the drug business. Rojas was a survivor and had joined the TCPLM to escape his dismal surroundings and to live what he perceived to be an exciting lifestyle as a cartel member.

He had moved up through the ranks in the organization and was chosen to be Sergio's right-hand man due to his intelligence, and loyalty. He had supported Rojas at every step along the way, despite his disdain for the brutal tactics that had made him rich and powerful. In truth, he despised Rojas for his inhuman actions, and in particular, for his treatment of Lusia Gaicia.

Ramirez had been smitten with her since Rojas kidnapped her from the small, poor village in Columbia. She was a teenager when Rojas moved her into his home and made her his sex slave and his lover. He had beaten her repeatedly and had forced her to have an abortion when she had become pregnant.

He had brought her to Caracas when he opened a new office there. She worked for him in the office handling the scheduling and distribution routes of the supply lines of cocaine from Columbia through Venezuela to the Dominican Republic.

The TCPLM was in partnership with the Venezuelan government. The whole country was involved in drogas, drugs. The military, the cartel drug dealers, called the traficante de drogas, were all in business together. It was a totally corrupt association. Luisa was an efficient worker in the TCPLM and was in the center of the operation due to her job duties and her association, awful as it was for her, with Rojas.

Ramirez had been in love with her from the first time he had seen her and hated Rojas for his treatment of her. Diego was possessed by the idea of being with her.

As he looked at her empty desk he thought of an incident where Rojas had belittled her in the office. He remembered it verbatim as it had related to Luisa spending time with the American baseball player Harold Gatewood, a man Ramirez truly hated.

Hal Graff

Rojas had summoned Luisa into his office and immediately, a shouting match had burst forth. Ramirez mentally replayed the entire conversation.

Rojas was the first to speak. "Luisa, I know what you are up to. You will never again see that man."

She had answered, "I will see him whenever I want Sergio."

"No, I will not allow that."

"I have a life. I intend to live it as I see fit."

"You belong to me."

"I don't belong to anyone."

"You are mine."

"No, you want to control me."

"I forbid you to see him."

"I will see him."

"I told you I would kill your family if you ever tried to leave me."

"You will not do that."

"Why not ?"

"Because if you do that it that would cause me to hate you more than I do now."

"I swear I will kill them."

"Then I will leave."

"I will never let you do that. You will stay here."

"You have many women."

"I still own you."

"I am not a trophy or a bird you can keep in a cage."

"You know I can be very dangerous."

"You have beaten me and raped me for years. That is why I hate you."

Love and Death in the Dominican Republic

"I will rape you again."

"Then I will hate you even more."

"I will beat you with my belt."

"It will do you no good. I would rather be dead than be with you."

"A good beating has always made you see the light."

"It is useless Sergio. I do not care to live if you continue to force me to stay."

"You have no place to go."

"I will find a place. I will be happy anywhere as long as I am away from you."

"It is the American, the ballplayer, Harold Gatewood, isn't it ?"

"Yes. He is wonderful. But, I decided to leave you years ago. I need to get out of this prison in which you have me confined."

"I saw you eating lunch with him every day last week."

"Yes. It was fantastic to be with him."

"I watched you go dancing."

"Yes, it was great fun."

"And, you went to the movies with him."

"Of course, I want to be with him every minute of the day."

"I saw you go to his hotel. I know you stayed with him until the next morning."

"Yes I did. We made love many times. He is kind, and the best lover I have had in my whole life."

"I made love to you."

"No, you forced me to have sex with you. There is a big difference."

"I am a great lover."

"No, you are a disgusting pig. You don't measure up to him in any way."

"I can kill him."

"That would only make me want to kill you."

"I forbid you to see him again."

"Stay away from me Sergio. I will do what I want. And, I will be with him whenever I want."

After her final comment of rebellion, with tears streaming down her face, Luisa walked to the women's lounge to compose herself. Ramirez had said to her, "I am sorry you had to go through that. I feel sorry for you Luisa. Sergio has treated you like dirt for years."

Ramirez shook his head as he remembered what had happened after the incident. She had spent the night with Gatewood. In the morning she had returned to her apartment to get ready for work. Sergio Rojas had shown up unannounced and proceeded to beat her unmercifully. She had arrived at the office wearing sunglasses to cover her blacken eyes, and a sweater to cover the bruises on her arms.

Ramirez had vowed that he would always treat her nicely if she would move in with him. He loved her with all of her heart. As much as he hated Gatewood for what had transpired after he killed Sergio Rojas, Ramirez was glad his employer had met his maker.

After Rojas's death, Ramirez had rescued Luisa from the farm where the monster had beaten and nearly killed her. Diego had taken her to the clinic near the TCPLM training camp in the mountains and had returned to bring her back to Caracas once she had recovered. He had found out that she had left to make her way to America to be with Gatewood.

Ramirez had killed the doctor who had released her. After being given false information by the doctor, he had set out to find her, but had initially been sent in the wrong direction. Once his path had been corrected he had always been one step behind her on her journey through Columbia, Panama, Belize, Costa Rica, and Mexico. She had proceeded on to America with Gatewood, where she met her death.

His hatred for Gatewood had developed into an out-of-control obsession. Someday, he would find the ballplayer and kill him.

Ramirez's thoughts returned to the purpose of the meeting today. He was to discuss the interruption of the supply lines through the Dominican Republic for the drug cartels. Two leaders of the Columbian drug cartels and one crime family head in Venezuela would be guests at the meeting.

Diego Ramirez proceeded to review his assessments of each leader, starting with Lino Pascual, perceived head of the Montanas las Productores, the Mountain Producers cartel. Contacts with the cartel were made with Pascual, but the real man behind the throne was unknown. Whoever he was, he had managed to keep his identity secret.

Lino had ascended to be the front man of the cartel when his brother Ruben was arrested, extradited to America by the Columbian government, and convicted on charges under the racketeering influenced and corruption organizations program, the RICO act. The RICO law allowed America to bring leaders of foreign criminal organizations to trail. Ruben was still in jail and was expected to maintain that address for many years.

The Mountain Producers cartel was still the strongest drug producing organization in Columbia despite Ruben's conviction, and the unknown factor of Lino's desire to wrestle control of the cartel from the true man behind the scenes, Mateo Amon. Also unknown was the hatred Amon had for Gatewood as his daughter Sofia had died when she was hiking with Gatewood in Ella Se Cayo, Venezuela.

One of the Mountain Producer's biggest strengths was the fact that they operated in the mountains, in the think jungle, and enjoyed the support of the locals, many of whom were still being paid by the cartel to grow cocaine. They were a guerilla organization with deep ties to the area.

The Columbian military had not been able to dent their organization. Their network used producers who were loyal, and felt a kinship with the organization. The cartel members lived like animals in the jungle. They were a tough bunch, a true adversary of the Columbian government.

Ramirez also thought that they were a very good customer and that they would be receptive to his suggestions, as they used the TCPLM as their first choice for marketing their cocaine.

The second Columbia cartel at the meeting would be the Carmelo cartel, headed by Rafael Carmelo, the Hombre del Carmelo. His nickname meant the "candy man." He heads the crime family that has paid the TCPLM handsomely to bribe our military and politicians here in Venezuela for our distribution systems. He is also a good customer.

We are still using some of the older distribution routes to move some of his product. We are still moving cocaine from Columbia to here, then to Central America, then Mexico, and finally into the United States.

Carmelo has friends in the Central American and Mexican governments that work with him. He also pays large bribes to the United States border agents to allow shipments to cross into the Southwestern states. He knows which agents can be corrupted.

Ramirez knew the American border patrol had many good people who had their hands tied by the American president but Carmelo could get to the bad apples and move his product across their border.

Ramirez knew that it was a pity that the American politicians had not enforced their borders. Their inaction had resulted in a business boom for the TCPLM. The last eight years had been open season for drugs, and terrorists, to move into the United States.

Hal Graff

We could not have placed a more beneficial person for us in their White House as they did when they elected the feckless one many years ago. The whole world was laughing at him. But, Ramirez knew he should not look negatively at such a wonderful, unexpected gift that had been dropped into their lap.

Ramirez was aware that the original distribution route through Central America and Mexico into the United States was somewhat secure in its operation at the present time. The real problem to be discussed in the meeting today was the stability of the Venezuelan government and their reduced capacity to protect the distribution system from the country to the Caribbean countries of Cuba, Hatti, and the Dominican Republic, and the United States territory of Puerto Rico.

The cooperation of the Bertalina government in Cuba had been lessened since the failure of the attempted coup by now-deceased General Domingo. Ramirez hoped that he could entice Cuba to come back into the fold. He was well aware that Bertalina's friendship with the American baseball player Harold Gatewood had complicated Cuba's business relationship with the TCPLM. He viewed it as another good reason to kill Gatewood.

The last member to be in attendance at the meeting was the head of the largest crime family in Venezuela, Fabbri Durante. He was the member most impacted by the interruption of the supply lines to the Dominican Republic. Durante had close ties with his fellow Sicilian crime families and supplied most of the drugs that went to Europe. Spain, France, England, Belgium, and the rest of Europe were dependent on the Durante family to deliver cocaine for street usage. His shipments to America were also being curtailed.

The Durante crime family was losing vast amounts of money every day due to the interruption of deliveries, and Ramirez expected Fabbri Durante to be the most upset of his three guests.

Ramirez's thoughts were interrupted by news that all three of his guests were present. He welcomed each man as they arrived. Pascual, Carmelo, and Durante were ushered into the meeting room. The conversation started cordially as each man took a seat.

Rafael Carmelo, sat motionless in front of the Ramirez. He was a handsome man, with movie star looks, and an air of confidence that bordered on conceit. He was immaculately dressed, and wore enough gold jewelry to pass for an Olympic athlete who had won five gold medals.

He was a ladies man, with a girl in every port. He eyed everyone in the room with caution and was uncomfortable being in Caracas with his cocaine rivals. He had agreed to the TCPLM's previous distribution and protection terms but he had always followed a success plan that was founded on the principle of trusting no one and remaining cautious.

Lino Pascual was seated on Ramirez's right, next to Diaz and Emilo. While Pascual was not the true head of the Mountain Producers cartel he played the part well. He was dressed conservatively, like a

Hal Graff

businessman, in a beige-colored suit, beige shirt, brown tie with white dots, brown socks, and a pair of highly-shined brown slip-on shoes.

He was of how a typical Columbian looed in terms of his skin and hair color, facial hair, dark eyes, and straight, white teeth. He too was suspicious of the purpose of the meeting and was looking forward to hearing the details of the program.

Fabbri Durante was seated on Ramirez's left. He was nervous, and shifted his body continuously in his seated position, as if his pants were sticking to the chair's seat, and that his movement would give him freedom. He could have played a part in a Hollywood mafia movie, as he had the look of a gangster.

His olive skin, dark eyes, heavy eyebrows, and stocky build were stereotypical Italian. He was bald, with long hair on the sides head pulled back into a small ponytail at the back of his head. His persona was that of a mean man, and it was accurate.

Ramirez continued, "My friends, we are here today to talk about the status of the interruption of our cocaine trafficking business to the Dominican Republic and through Mexico. Several factors are impacting our efforts. As you can see, the representatives of the Nazoa government are not present as their stability will be a topic of our meeting, which will be confidential."

All three members reported that they had spoken with President Nazoa about the problems in his government and were brought up to date about his actions to improve the situation in the county.

Love and Death in the Dominican Republic

"I am glad that you have talked to the president. We all want him to remain in office to stabilize our business relationship, which has been positive and cooperative over the years. We all have an understanding with Nazoa. We pay him to keep the military on our good side, and to assist our shipments of drugs to our locations outside of the country."

"It has been a good association. I asked you here today to discuss how we can make that situation permanent and to assure you that we have made improvements in our services for you, our customers, and partners."

All three guests voiced concerns over the recent disclosure of the distribution routes and receiving points in receiving countries that operated as a shipping base to America and Europe.

"Gentlemen, our mole, Ms. Luisa Gaicia, who worked in our office, and forwarded the operational details to Harold Gatewood and the CIO, has been killed in America. The internal problem that was one of the causes of the recent interrupted supply deliveries has been corrected. I have reworked our delivery routes to countries outside Venezuela, and have had our receiving bases moved to different locations. We have solved that problem."

The news was met with open arms, relief, and also a warning that all three of the guests would not tolerate another such incident. They lost vast amounts of money during the disruption period. They wanted assurance that no other disloyal employees could cause such a similar occurrence again.

"You have that assurance from me. Any employee who acts in such a manner will be instantly killed. Also, I have initiated a backup system of checks and balances in our system that did not exist before. My predecessor, Sergio Rojas, was romantically involved with Ms. Gaicia, and did not check on her work or her loyalty. That will not happen with me in charge."

The three guests seemed to agree with Ramirez's guarantee. They wanted to know what Nazoa had told him in order to make sure each of them were being told the same story.

"Nazoa also told me that he has staved off a public recall that would certainly led to his removal from office. He also stated he has shored up his political base and is in no danger of impeachment. He is arresting and disposing off his political opponents and has control of his political destiny."

All three asked about the state of the country's economy.

"I was assured that the public is now somewhat reassured that better times are ahead. He has raised the minimum wage six times this year to appease the public's fear of runaway inflation. Most encouraging was his statement that the Middle East Oil Carte Countries Organization, MEOCCO, has agreed to limit production, starting with a twenty-five percent reduction in drilling. The reduced supply will help raise the price of oil and bring money into the national treasury."

All three guests wanted to know about the other internal supply problems of food and medicine.

"The military is handling the distribution of food and medicine. Apart from some good, old-fashioned, black-marketing action by the military, that problem appears to be under control. And, after all gentlemen, we would also engage in a little black-marketing if we were in their shoes."

Pascual, Carmelo, and Durante all wanted to know about the mass immigration from the country to Columbia, Brazil, the Central Americas, Europe, and America.

"I was assured that even though it looks bad, it is a good thing, as the most disgruntled people are leaving. The result is a remaining population is one that can more easily controlled with iron-fisted tactics if need be."

All three men wanted to know how their shipments could continue if Nazoa was forced from power.

"Then we will reinstitute the Venezuelan way, the way of corruption, which characterizes the country. We bought Nazoa and we will buy the next person in charge if we need to."

All agreed that that option sounded reasonable but wanted to know what path they should plan as a backup option if a do-gooder like Leal Servidor in Mexico took power.

Hal Graff

"We need to plan for that contingency. But, accidents do happen, even to do-gooder presidents. A person such as that will have to fight the inbred corruption of the Venezuelan political and economic systems. We can outlast such a person if one would become president."

Fabbri Durante spoke up with a concern. "As we all know, I have been most impacted by the supply line interruption to the Dominican Republic because most all of my drug supply goes to Europe. I will not allow my operation to be compromised due to outside interference. I will take matters into my own hands and eliminate anyone who stands in my way."

"How would you plan to do that Fabbri ?"

"Obviously, my Sicilian contacts would send someone talented in the art of trash removal to correct the situation."

Pascual, Carmelo, and Ramirez all gave the green light to Durante to take whatever action needed to protect his interests, as they would all do the same if they were in his position. They all also pledged to help if needed.

They meeting ended on a positive note in terms of approaching the reinstitution of the supply lines. As the meeting was about to break up, Durante said he had one more item to bring up for discussion. "I have noticed that one man's name continues to come up in our discussion of what and who has caused us problems. It is always America that sticks their nose into our business, and the name of a seemingly unassuming baseball player, Harold Gatewood, pops up. I want all of you to know that I will not bow to either. I will kill him if he interferes with us again."

Diego Ramirez turned his head away from his guests so that they would not see the smile on his face. He snickered and said, "If I can't kill Gatewood myself then maybe Durante's Sicilian buddies can do it for me."

Chapter 3

"I am the last of seven"

August 21

EKAIN KOLDO STAGGERED FROM HIS BED to the bathroom, splashed cold water on his face, and looked into the mirror. He was horrified. He used to be a handsome man, with dark black hair, eyes, and mustache. Now, his hair and mustache were gray, his eyes were cursed with bags below the sockets, and his face was sprouting worry lines that had turned into deep-set wrinkles.

He had lost weight and was gaunt in his appearance. He had lost his former uproarious sense of humor, and was now short-tempered, and surly with his wife, friends, and coworkers. The couple had lost long-time friends due to his now-volatile temper. He was impossible to live with. A good night's sleep was a distant memory.

He had grown up on a farm outside La Merdedur De Serpant, Spain, near the beautiful Pyrenees mountains. He was the youngest of seven brothers. Four brothers had died in during World War II when Franco gave Germany the green light to bomb the area. Two brothers died later fighting in the AIO underground for

Love and Death in the Dominican Republic
independence and self-determination for the Basque people.

After the war, Koldo graduated from law school and set up a practice in Madrid. He thrived and had become ridiculously wealthy. He followed his brothers' actions and joined the AIO. He worked in many capacities for the organization, and was appointed to the national committee as its legal consul. He moved into the position of deputy national commander and was elected as national commander where he had served for twenty-three years.

He was a loyal, dedicated servant of the Basque people and the AIO. His association with the AIO was confidential, not even known by his wife.

Koldo showered, walked downstairs to the kitchen, kissed his wife, and sat down at the table. His wife brought a traditional Basque breakfast to the table.

"Dear, here is your favorite breakfast. I have fixed you brandade, which is salt cod cooked in olive oil, fried potatoes, cherries, and coffee."

Koldo was distracted, lost in his thoughts about the problems of the AIO, and did not respond to his wife.

"Ekain, did you hear me ?"

"I am sorry. What did you say ?"

"I said I have fixed you your favorite breakfast."

"Thank you."

"Are you alright ? You seem so distracted lately."

"I was just thinking about my brothers. I am the last of seven. The rest are dead."

His wife walked to the table and kissed him. "I know it is very painful for you Ekain. You know you must go on."

He took her hand and said, "I know." He then finished his breakfast and drove to AIO national headquarters.

The routine of the meetings had almost become depressing to him, as they rehashed old problems, old enemies, and old battles. He had helped the AIO fight the same situations for years but little progress had been made. In fact, the Basque people's quest for independence and self-determination had lost ground in many respects during his tenure. He was tired, and it showed in his appearance.

Twelve men, loyal patriots at heart, had come to the national headquarters to promote AIO operations that would protect their members and further the goals of the Basque people of Northern Spain and Southwestern France.

Each meeting had seen the committee members say their helloes, and take their appropriate seats at a large rectangular-shaped table. They would all gaze at the wall above the chair at the far end of the table and look at the red, green and white flag of the Basque people. Each meeting, the tall, once black-haired, mustachioed man who was the national commander would rise from his chair and speak the same words.

"Welcome fellow freedom fighters. Long Live the Basque people."

"Thank you Sir. We salute you."

To some of the committee members he looked even older than he was at the last meeting, with more gray hair invading his sideburns and around the tops of his ears. His face was drawn even more than in the past, and when he spoke his voice was not as strong as before."

"His spirit had plunged after suffering several hits over the last several years, the timeframe in which their hated enemy, Harold Gatewood, had entered their sphere of operation. Failure of one operation after another had accentuated his passage from black hair into gray.

Their leader would always open the ask the scribe to note the presence of the five Regional Commanders, their Assistant Regional Commanders, the Assistant National Commander, and himself, Ekain Koldo, the National Commander."

Koldo would always say, "With our attended members, all three areas of our AIO organization are represented. Those areas are our logistics, political, and military divisions."

Then each member would nod their heads to acknowledge each of the division representatives.

The national commander would then call for the reports with the same words, "Tonight, we continue our long struggle for self-determination, establishment of our country borders, the free use of our language, and the enjoyment of our proud culture. May we always be free, never again to suffer the indignities forced upon us by the dictator Franco."

Then, in a display of support ten pairs of hands would pound the table in approval of the National Commander's comments.

Then, on cue, Koldo would say, "Our meeting tonight will include reports from all divisions, and the discussion on another proposed operation of revenge. Would the regional commander in charge of membership please read his report ?"

The regional commander would then give the report. Usually, the membership numbers would have declined due to the dissatisfaction with the results caused by the most recent failure to eliminate the one person most responsible for the continued embarrassment of the AIO terrorist organization, Harold Gatewood.

Additional demoralizing results, and disgrace, would be added when the failure of the agents who had met their demise at Gatewood's hands would be announced. Usually, the younger members of the AIO, the twenty-to-thirty age group, would be demanding retaliatory action be taken against Harold Gatewood, whom everyone considered a symbol of the failure to successfully advance the mission for Basque independence.

Koldo would then ask for the financial report. The results were usually the same, with finances declining due to losses in our membership dues and our poor results in the revenue producing areas."

Next in the regular routine would be the report from the regional commander of the political division, who would have to deliver the bad news efforts in the political arena have additional shown additional backward movement.

The cause was always the same. The commander's words could be recited from memory. "The world community still continues to label the AIO a terrorist organization due to our use of violence, and the failed missions in the recent past as previously mentioned. Also, we have suffered terrible criticism related to the attempts to kill Harold Gatewood."

After agreeing with the cause of the decline, Koldo would always state that after trying a political approach, a more peaceful outreach by the AIO for a cease fire of our military actions had failed.

He would also mention that the AIO had offered to disband if its members could be granted independence and our goal of self-determination in the areas our people have lived in for centuries. The result was always the same, as all offers would have been rejected.

Koldo would then ask for the progress report in the area in of prisoner's rights. All efforts to secure better living conditions, the end of torture, and a plea to not house our patriots in prisons which are far spread out from each other would also have failed. Political gains would always be described in terms as short-term steps forward because they could be reversed when elections resulted in a change of political leadership, and ideologies.

The next routine step would be to discuss the military arm of the organization. More demands for military action and training were always demanded by the membership. The improvements at the training camp in Northern Spain would also be on every meeting agenda.

Eventually, every meeting would return to a discussion of a vote on a possible military style action on a well-known target, one who deserved, and needed to be, eliminated, Harold Gatewood. The details of the latest operation would be discussed and a vote for approval would always be taken and approved.

Gatewood had been a tough enemy who had refused to go down. The frustration he had caused the AIO damages to all areas of the organization's activities. All twelve members were numb to the numerous failures to eliminate him. Tonight, everyone was hoping this mission would be the one to successfully accomplish that task.

This evening, Koldo would review the mission that had been discussed and previously approved. "Comrades, the question to be decided is if this military action, called Operation Slice and Dice, should be placed in action through the appointment of the field agent who will perform the mission. The subject to be sliced and diced is Gatewood. "

Discussion on the pros and cons of the organization's increased use of more violent actions, and the approval or rejection of the plan, were again discussed for a few tense minutes. The vote was taken, and the result was announced.

Koldo would then continue, "My friends, I am pleased to announce that the mission is approved by a near-unanimous vote. The deputyt national commander and I would like to now address the assignment of the operative to be assigned to the mission, and discuss the strategy and tactics required to successfully accomplish our task."

"We all agree. Let's proceed."

"Fellow patriots, we have suffered a reduction in our field operative area due to the deaths of Aitor Lehoi and Gabirel Domeka, when Mr. Gatewood led the CIO and the local police authorities to the Lehoi estate in an arrest mission."

"We also lost Andoni Mikola when he tried to kill Gatewood at the airport."

"Yes, he was a rising star in our organization. We miss him. We need to settle the score with Mr. Gatewood on that matter also."

"We all agree on that Sir."

"He has been a thorn in our side for too long."

"We also lost one of our best field agents when Bakar Kemen was killed at the Havana airport while attempting to eliminate Gatewood before he and his finance Christina Abene left the country."

"Yes, that was another embarrassment."

"We also lost his brother Bittor Kemen in Tokyo when he was thrown off the rooftop by the CIO agent assigned to protect Gatewood.

"We thought we had the ideal candidate for our operation in Beijing, China in Eneko Itzal. He had been through all of our training, excelling in all phases of the program. He had field experience and had performed a series of political blackmailing missions against five politicians in the Spanish government who would not pay us to keep their affairs with married woman confidential."

"Yes, he was a good agent. He was not opposed to killing. But, he also failed to eliminate Gatewood. "

"Comrades, we need someone fearless, and not afraid to do whatever is needed. When I visited our elite agent training camp before our last failed attempted removal of Gatewood in Korea we had three men and one woman who were at the top of our field force. We chose Misio Hilketa. His cover as a mime was ingenious but he was killed by Gatewood during the attempted removal."

"Yes Sir, he came from a family which has been loyal to our cause for many years. The family had sent two relatives to contribute as field operatives. He believed in the AIO goal of self-determination and independence and wanted to contribute in any way he could."

"He was loyal, and also brought a desire for revenge against Gatewood."

"Yes Sir, his cousins were Bakar and Bittor Kemen, who were assigned to eliminate the American when he was in Cuba, and Tokyo, Japan."

"He sounded like a man with the blood lust we need for this mission. Even his Basque name had a meaning that implied he would perform wonderfully. His name meant my shadow."

"Yes Sir, he came close to killing Gatewood but fell short when he was shot."

"Comrades, we had a qualified candidate who we believed was our best agent for Operation Wood Chopper. She was Usoa Hilketa. Her name meant the "dove of murder". She was Misio's sister. She was a vastly talented agent, with skills in all areas. While I appreciated the special skills a woman agent could bring to the table in this business, I wanted a man to handle the South Korea mission. I did not choose her for that particular mission because Gatewood was used to being with women who possessed world-class physical beauty. She had the skills but was a plain-looking woman. That comment was not a criticism of her."

Koldo gain continued, "The target, Harold Gatewood, is a handsome, charming, exciting man who draws the most beautiful women in the world to him like moths to a light. She would not have been able to get close enough to him to carry out the mission. She understood and pledged to be ready if she were called on to carry out a mission in the future. She stayed ready and was patient. But, she also failed in her mission to kill Gatewood in Venezuela."

Many on the committee had grown tired of Koldo's repetition of past events, which prompted one member to say, "Sir, thank you for reviewing the history of our agent's efforts. Where is Gatewood now ?"

Koldo stated that Gatewood was now in Mexico, scouting Mexican baseball. He added, "Gentlemen, we need to eliminate him now. I had chosen an agent to be considered for Operation Slice and Dice. He was Sandalio La Muerte. He was a ruthless, aggressive warrior."

A question had arisen about his background.

"He had gone through our training program and has performed admirably in the field. He gleefully performed contract hits. He had no vices or mental problems that would prevent him accomplishing the mission. I urged the committee to approve him for the mission."

Koldo's recommendation did the trick and Sandalio La Muerte, the "True Wolf of Death" was charged with killing the AIO's main nemesis, Harold Gatewood. Unfortunately, for the AIO, and La Murete, he met his death at the hands of CIO operative Darren Fuller while the "True Wolf of Death" was trying to shoot Gatewood in Mexico City.

All committee members wished for a different type of meeting today, and their wishes were granted.

Koldo spoke, "My fellow patriots, I am happy you are here today. We have two topics to discuss today."

Everyone was stunned by the change in routine. They remained hopeful that new ground could be broken today.

"First, we have suffered a dramatic reduction in income due to the severe reduction in our supply of drugs from Columbia. The supply lines from Venezuela to the Dominican Republic had been compromised by a leak in the TCPLM office in

Caracas. Their organization has taken corrective steps to develop new drop off locations, and new delivery routes and drop zones for the cocaine in the La Merdedur de Serpant area of Northern Spain."

The committee members pounded the table in glorious approval.

"I am assured that the supply lines will be effective and that drugs will start to flow into the Dominican Republic and then into Northern Spain."

A question was raised about how the leak in the TCPLM office was corrected.

"The mole, Luisa Gaicia, has been terminated. She was killed in America, where she had fled with our old buddy Harold Gatewood to start a new life together."

All in attendance agreed that the TCPLM had done the right thing and were thankful that the supply lines would again be open.

"Gentlemen, the TCPLM did not kill her. She was shot by a deranged woman, a stalker who is in love with Gatewood."

The room went silent.

"We are thankful for her actions. We would have hoped she would have killed Gatewood also. But, perhaps she will do that for us in the future."

All members agreed that Gatewood should get the punishment by death that he deserved.

"The good news is that we will have a stable flow of drug money again coming in that we can use for street sales and to use for blackmail purposes on the Spanish politicians and businessmen who need to hide their corruption and affairs."

The committee members hooted with glee. A question then arose. "What is the second topic Ekain ?"

"I am glad you asked that question. Another person has also contributed greatly to the supply problem that has cost us much money. He made matters worse for President Nazoa in Venezuela and killed the head of the TCPLM, Sergio Rojas, in Caracas. He is our constant source of disruption, Harold Gatewood."

All members demanded to know what Ekain Koldo was going to do about their enemy.

"I am asking for permission to form a plan, called Operation Shelf Life, which will train our best agent for the task of eliminating Gatewood once and for all."

All members pounded the table and demanded a solution that had evaded them in all previous attempts."

"I propose to go to our training camp in Northern Spain outside of La Merdedur De Serpant, and choose the agent, man or woman, who can accomplish the mission. Even though we have tried to kill Gatewood many times, his luck will soon run out. Sooner or later, he will appear somewhere that will cause us problems. His imprint is stamped on most of our failures in the last several years."

A question arose. "What will be different this time ?"

"We will have a head start on the specific training needed to take out Gatewood, wherever he pops up and interferes with our operation. That is why I am calling

Love and Death in the Dominican Republic

this mission Operation Self Life, because the killing of Gatewood will not expire, unlike a can of vegetables that has an expiration date of its shelf life. Our commitment to Gatewood will be renewed again and will never expire. This time, we will get him."

Discussion followed on the topic, and the specific details required for an agent to be trained in any type of environment where the mission would need to be carried out.

"My fellow patriots, do you want to approve the mission ?"

Resounding cries of "Yes !" filled the air and the mission was approved.

"Wonderful. The mission is approved. I will go to La Merdedur De Serpant soon and work with our training commander about the program. I will also review the strengths and weaknesses of our current cadre of agents, and return with a recommendation for the committee."

Cries of hope filled the air, as the success of the mission was long overdue.

"Thank you my comrades. I will keep you updated on our progress. We will be ready when Gatewood again becomes another problem for our organization. Long live the Basque people and their quest for self-determination and freedom !"

Chapter 4

Single Malt Whisky

August 22

FABBRI DURANTE SETTLED INTO HIS WINDOW SEAT, number 3A in first class, and buckled his seat belt. He was ready to relax for his sixteen hour flight from Caracas, Venezuela to Palermo, Sicily. He leaned back and closed his eyes, trying to make up for a long night of worry, and little sleep.

He had not been back to Palermo for many years. He had left the Durante crime family in a huff, after a falling out with his brother, Celestino. He had served as the crime family as the capo bastone, the underboss, for his older brother, the capofamiglia, the head of the family. Each had a different view of how to run the business.

His brother always took a more vicious approach to business matters and the muscling out of rival crime families. Celestino's approach was centered on a shoot-first-and-ask-questions later ideology. Fabbri preferred to use more finesse and diplomacy. However, he was not adverse to using violence if the need arose.

It became clear to everyone that one of the two brothers had to leave Palermo. Fabbri was the one who pulled up roots and moved to Caracas to run the family's business in Venezuela. He successfully built up his own operation in Caracas, becoming a powerful capofamiglia himself. Despite their differences the two factions of the original family business worked closely with each other in the drug business, even though they had not seen each other for years.

Fabbri's rest was interrupted by the soothing, soft voice of the female flight attendant who served first class. "Sir, would you like a pillow and blanket ?"

"Yes, please, that would be very nice."

"Would you also like something to drink ?"

"Yes, please bring me a Vanducci single malt whisky, on the rocks."

"Yes Sir. You mad an excellent choice."

"Yes. It was judged the world's best whisky this year."

"Yes I heard that."

"It is distilled in Palermo, Sicily."

"I will bring it to you right away Sir."

"Thank you."

After the pretty flight attendant left, Fabbri again rested his head on the headrest of his seat, closed his eyes, and thought about the drink he was about to be served. The drink was brewed in Italy, and aged in a cask, a wooden barrel. The brewing and aging process was done in one location, which is what separated it from other types of the drink that used multiple locations to complete the process.

Fabbri's knowledge of the whisky business had been a life-long joy. He was also a regular user of the product. He liked single malt whisky because it was distilled from one malt, and used a fermented mash from a malted grain, typically barley, corn, or rye, in the process. In the single malt distilling process the enzymes in the malt, the starches, were broken down into sugars.

He was a world-class connoisseur of the beverage, and agreed whole-heartedly with the Latin phrase that the distilling process for single malt whisky created agua vitae, the water of life. For many years, he had served on the rating board that picked the world's best whisky each year in Naples, Italy.

Fabbri laughed when he thought of his experiences as a whisky judge. A judge used over twenty criteria to rate each whisky that vied for the title of the world's best. His knowledge about whisky had brought him fame, and pleasure. He was especially adept at judging each entry by using his sight, sense of smell, and taste, buds.

Even though he had had his differences with his brother, he was proud of Celestino this year because he had taken his advice on how to make money in the judging process. Fabbri had told him how to bribe enough judges to swing the title to the Vanducci distillery, which earned him a handsome kickback of a lump sum amount of money and a royalty on each bottle sold.

The flight attendant arrived with his drink, and Fabbri opened his eyes, said thank you, and sipped the agua vitae into his mouth, swirled it around, and swallowed it. It felt so good going down, and warmed his mouth and throat. He relished what was, for him, one of life's greatest pleasures. He finished his drink, closed his eyes, and napped until the plane landed in Palermo. He walked to the baggage claim area, grabbed his suitcase, and walked out of the terminal into the hot Sicilian sunshine. He stopped and closed his eyes, letting the sunshine bake his face, and further tan his face.

He was home again. His move to Venezuela had been a good one as it had allowed him to escape his differences with Celestino, and allowed him to build and control his own family. But, Sicily was always in his blood, beckoning him to return. He opened his eyes and saw his brother standing by the car on the street that ran in front of the terminal.

Fabbri and Celestino walked toward each other, stopped, threw their arms each other, kissed each other on each cheek, and smiled.

Celestino broke the ice and said, "It is nice to see you again Fabbri. It has been too long."

"Yes, it has been sixteen years since I was last in Palermo."

Fabbri was dismayed at his brother's appearance. He was very portly, tipping the scale at three-hundred-fifteen pounds. His hair had thinned, and his waistline had greatly expanded. He spoke in a gruff voice that was always one of his trademarks. His breathing was labored and loud, which was caused by his weight problem.

He was impeccably dressed in a white suit, white shirt, white tie, white hat with a white brim, and white shoes. He accented his appearance with a white walking stick that sported a white ivory head.

The difference in appearance between the two brothers was stark. Fabbri was thin, in good shape, had a healthy complexion, and had eyes that were aware and piercing. He looked as if he could compete in ironman triathlon event in his age bracket.

After laughing about the coup Celestino had pulled off in the whisky judging world, the two brothers hopped in the car, with Fabbri in the back seat. They were driven by a tall, lean Italian man wearing a blue chauffer's cap who Celestino called "the wheel man".

On the way to the compound Fabbri asked how the family business was functioning. Celestino said that the organization was growing due to a competent consigliere advisor, a capable capo bastone underboss, a stable of talented caporegime leaders, and loyal, ruthless bands of soldati soldiers. The organizational structure resembled other crime families such as the Yakuza in Japan, and the Russian mobs.

He mentioned that the territory of operations had been expanded to include units in Italy, the United Kingdom, Germany, Canada, Australia, Argentina, Brazil, Columbia, and Africa.

Celestino said the activities and revenue streams of the family, the La Costa Nostra, still included protection rackets, vote buying, smuggling, bid rigging, loan sharking, racketeering, fraud, extortion, assault, weapons sales, prostitution, money laundering, fencing stolen property, robbery, contract killing, and of course drug sales.

He also said, "We still use the old ways Fabbri. We have a code of conduct, an initiation ceremony that include a blood oath, and a pecking order where members of equal status refer to each other as a compare, and where unequal members great their superiors, a padrino, with respect. We still follow the omerta, the code of silence when it comes to family business."

He continued, "Our members are violent, and commit murder, but they are also men of honor who value their reputation and have a prideful respect for the family, and have a sense of brotherhood."

Celestino was on a roll and Fabbri did not want to interrupt him.

"All of the men follow the rules of the code of conduct. They know that they must be loyal, rational, honorable, and that they need to keep their eyes and ears open and their mouth shut when it comes to the family. They need to have class, not chase another family member's wife or disrespect a fellow family member, not associate with the police, always be available for duty, treat their own wives with respect, always tell the truth to their superiors, not steal from the family, and not kill other family members unless it is unavoidable."

The car rolled to a stop at the family compound and the brothers piled out and entered the front door.

Fabbri asked if he could go to his room for a short nap to relax. After his nap, they met in the parlor before supper for a glass of Vanducci single-malt whisky. During supper the brothers feasted on a meal of spaghetti al la carbonara made with pasta noodles, eggs, cheese, bacon, pork, goose meat, and pepper, salad greens, and Marsala red wine. The meal was topped off with Sicilian cassata cake.

After supper they returned to the parlor to discuss business, and to enjoy another shot of Vanducci whisky.

"Fabbri, what news do you have for me about the supply lines from Venezuela ?"

"The TCPLM has ousted the mole in the Caracas office."

"Who was it ?"

"It as a woman named Luisa Gaicia. She had been Sergio Rojas' kept woman for years."

"You said had been, in the past tense."

"Yes. She is dead."

"How did she die ?"

"She fled the country, chasing after an American baseball player she loved. She was killed by one of his deranged groupies in the United States."

"Who is the ballplayer ?"

"The one who has been giving us trouble, Harold Gatewood."

"The one who has caused havoc in Venezuela ?"

"Yes. He is an aggravating character. He thinks he is some kind of international spy."

"Do you think we should kill him if he gets in our way again ?"

"Of course. We can't have him costing us money."

"When are the drug shipments to the Dominican Republic going to be fully operational again ?"

"Within the week. The TCPLM has changed the delivery routes, the schedules, and the drop points. They have weeded out and killed anyone else who was trying to skim the supply that was going into the Dominican Republic."

"Do you think they have the situation under control ?"

"Yes. Rafael Carmelo, Lino Pascual, of the Columbian drug producing organizations, and myself have made it clear to the TCPLM that we all need to be totally online again as soon as possible."

Do you think Carmelo or Pascual are plotting to take over part of our operation ?"

"No. I believe they are satisfied with their share and just want the routes to be operational again. We are most impacted by the slowdown in supply through the Dominican Republic. Most of Carmelo and Pascual's shipments are going through the traditional channels of Central America, Mexico, and into the Southwest United States."

"Are they getting cooperation from the Mexican government ?"

"That question is unanswered. As you now Leal Servidor is now the president since Alto Roble is dead.

Servidor wants to mend fences with America and crack down on the drug cartels."

"He should be careful or Salvador Masas, the Stinging Hornet, will kill him. Masas will not stand for less than one hundred percent protection from the Mexican government. He demands to get all the freedom to operate that he pays for."

"It will remain to be seen how that situation will play out. Servidor is a goody-two-shoes, and idealist who wants to change the drug culture."

"That approach will probably get him killed Fabbri."

"I agree. He should learn not to rock the boat."

"The news you bring is welcomed. I am looking forward to being fully operational soon."

"Celestino, let's have another round of Vanducci whisky. I want to talk to you about a topic we touched on earlier."

After the shots were poured and the glasses clicked to each other's good health, Fabbri Durante spoke. "We need to seriously prepare for the removal of Gatewood, or anyone else who gets in our way in the Dominican Republic."

"What do you want me to do ?"

"My brother, you are known as Il Balerino, because you dance on the graves of the enemies you send to Hell."

Celestino laughed heartedly and then agreed. "Yes, I am known for those actions."

Love and Death in the Dominican Republic

"I want you to provide a hitman, the toughest and best one you have, to take out Gatewood if he interferes with our business."

"I will."

"The other producers, Carmelo and Pascual are insisting that I provide that service if Gatewood shows up in the Dominican Republic, for any reason."

"They must hate him even more than we do."

"They do. Who do you have that can terminate him ?"

"I have the ideal man for the job. He is Baldovino Gioele. His nickname is Il Barbiere, the barber."

"Is he capable ?"

"Of course, or I would not keep him around. He is called the barber because of his special skills with a straight razor. He shaves off layers of skin on his victims before he kills them. He is a sadistic one."

"Baldovino the barber. He must have a lot of hair."

"That is the ironic part. He is as bald as a pool cue ball."

Both brothers broke out in laughter, then enjoyed another shot of Vanducci whisky. As Fabbri Durante headed to bed later in the evening he thought, "Things are breaking our way. If we run into any trouble Il Barbiere will take care of things."

Chapter 5

"No more jungle work"

September 10

GATEWOOD, FRESH FROM THE SHOWER, SLIPPED ON HIS BATHROBE, walked into the living room, clicked on the remote control to turn on the television and headed to the kitchen. He had not walked three steps until he heard a chilling news announcement.

"Susana Richards, the beautiful fugitive from justice, has just been placed on the CIO's most wanted list. Ms. Richards is wanted for the murders of three men, Gerald Atkinson, Grady Elliott, and Loren Melnor, who worked for the Placer De Los Lectores book publishing company in New York City. She is also wanted for the murder of Luisa Gaicia, the girlfriend of the well-known, former baseball player Harold Gatewood."

Gatewood paused a moment to think, and after brewing a cup of green tea, headed to his favorite chair in his living room. He sat down and thought about what he had just heard. At least the news station had been kind to Luisa, as they had not called her the former lover of Harold Gatewood. He was thankful for that courtesy. And, he was thankful they did not mention that the murder was committed in Gibson City, Illinois.

No word had been heard from Susana, and her whereabouts were totally unknown. He wondered where she was, and what evil deeds she was planning. He had lost much sleep over the past few weeks, worrying that she might turn unexpectedly. His thoughts were interrupted by another news flash on television.

"We bring you breaking information about Susana Richards, the beautiful young woman who is on the CIO's most wanted list for torturing and killing four people. Her car has been found and identified in a barn near her home town of Scalp, Minnesota. Her body was found burned beyond recognition inside the vehicle. Her body has been transferred to the Minnesota State Morgue for identification. We will bring you updates as the situation develops."

Gatewood's cell phone rang. "Hello, is this Mr. Harold Gatewood ?"

"Yes, this is he." After saying the words Harold laughed to himself about the time his high school English teacher had called his parents, when he had answered and responded to the same question in an incorrect grammatical manner. He had said, "Yes, this is him." His English teacher immediately corrected him on the phone by saying, "Oh no Harold. You must say this is he, not this is him."

Harold snapped out of his fog and answered listened to the caller's next question. This is the local news

Hal Graff

station from Bloomington, Illinois. Can we ask you for your thoughts on the breaking news report about Susana Richards' body being found in Minnesota ?"

"I would rather not comment on that matter. I prefer to let the police authorities handle the situation."

"We understand Mr. Gatewood. But, do you hold any animosity toward Susana for her killing of your girlfriend Luisa Gaicia ?"

"Again, I appreciate your call and know that you are only doing your job, but I do not have any facts on the situation and I really prefer not to comment."

"Will you tell us anything Harold ?"

"I wish you well, but I am not going to comment."

"Very well Harold. Thank you for your time."

"You're welcome."

Gatewood looked at the clock and thought, "it is only seven-thirty a.m. and the day is off to this kind of start."

Harold knew that the police had not identified the body, and prior to the morning's breaking news had no leads about Susana's movements or her location. Personally, he did not know what to make of the news report. He knew that Susana was capable of anything so he would only be sure she would be gone if he was looking down at her cold, dead body.

Harold had taken no chances after Susana had sped out of Gibson City after the murder. He had arranged for the Gibson City police and state trooper Alden Zorn to conduct drive-byes at his and his parents' homes at differing times of the day and night to make sure he and his parents were safe.

After his work in Korea for the CIO, he still enjoyed authorization to conceal and carry a weapon. Now, he always packed heat, even when he walked to and from his home to the workout building.

He also practiced his marksmanship by firing rounds at targets, red and blue plastic lids from small-sized food storage containers, which had been nailed to the largest tree behind his house. He had practiced his baseball footwork and throwing skills by throwing tennis balls at the same kinds of targets when he was a boy, and later as a professional player. He had secretly hoped that someday he would be able to enjoy that with his future grandsons.

Harold had feverishly been working out. He had been running, doing light weightlifting exercises, and hitting baseballs off batting tees into nets. He had built up his arm strength and was making positive progress.

To help his mental condition, which had taken another hit when Luisa was killed in his arms, he was meditating, and doing tai chi, taekwondo, and Brazilian jiu-jitsu exercises for strength, agility, and self-defense.

He was feeling better and had dedicated himself to becoming healthy in all areas, physically, mentally, and spiritually. He had appreciated the help his minister had given him the day when Luisa had died. He was also touched by the minister's graveside service for Luisa.

After setting his security alarm at his house each morning he would strap his pistol to his side and run two miles to the cemetery and visit Luisa's gravesite. On the return leg of the journey he always felt better, and more determined in his comeback attempt as a designated hitter.

Even though Susana Richards was presumed to be dead, he wondered if she were still alive. She could have easily changed her identity and physical appearance. People who could make those changes could easily be found and paid to make the old Susana disappear and the new one reappear.

A few hundred dollars could purchase a fake driver's license, a social security card, a voter's identification card, and a birth certificate. Illegal immigrants, and a president, had done it, and Susana was much more intelligent than they were.

Physically, she was beautiful, but plastic surgery could easily alter her looks and still retain her beauty, in another package. He had never met her, and had only seen the pictures of her she had sent to him. She could easily fool him if she had a desire to do so. He knew he had to be careful.

After returning from his four-mile run to and from the cemetery, Harold entered the house, reset the security alarm, poured himself a glass of cold water, and sat down in his favorite chair by the window in the family room.

He watched his friends, the birds and the squirrels, and again wondered what animals thought about as the scurried through their daily activities. He thought that their lives were easy compared to humans, as they were only concerned with having food and water, reproducing, and remaining safe. They did not have to worry about hitmen, drug cartels, dictators, the AIO, the Yakuza, and deranged female stalkers.

He envied them, and remembered when his life was much clearer, easier, and safer. He asked himself how he had evolved to this point. He was unsure, but he knew he wanted a new direction in his life.

His contemplation was interrupted by a phone call.

"Harold, this is Randle Quinn."

"Hi Randle."

"How are you ?"

"I am making progress."

"Good. Can I do anything for you ?"

"Yes, you can give me a new arm."

"I wish I could."

"Some agent you are Randle."

"I am glad you are teasing me. You must be getting better."

"Thanks. What do you have for me today ?"

"I wanted to see how you were feeling after the news about Susana Richards came out this morning."

"I am doing fine."

"Harold, I got a call from the scouting organization. They wanted to know how you are feeling, and if you would like to do some work for them again."

"That is very nice of them. I don't think I want to do anything for a while. I want to make sure my parents are safe and work on my comeback plans."

"Are you working out ?"

Hal Graff

"Yes, very diligently. I am making progress. But, keep that information under your hat."

"Harold, your doctoral dissertation research and the follow up scouting work has become the preferred model for everyone's scouting organization."

"Thanks."

"You have added supported research for players from all over the world. You have revolutionized how scouting is done."

"Thanks. The business is doing very well."

"Harold, if you want to go to work for them let me know. They love your work and will pay you top dollar."

"I don't think I want to do it right now Randle. Out of curiosity, what did they have in mind ?"

"They want you to scout the Winter leagues. Australia, Panama, and the Dominican republic have some prospects they want you to look at."

"Oh boy. I don't think I want to do another assignment outside the U.S.A. My first thought is to say no. I have had enough of that."

"Okay Harold. I don't blame you. I called to let you know they wanted to be sure you were doing alright and that the door is always open if you ever want to work for them again."

"Please tell them thanks for both thoughts."

"I will. Remember, don't be a stranger. Call me anytime. I can help, or if you want, talk about anything as friends."

"Thanks. I will."

Love and Death in the Dominican Republic

Gatewood clicked off his cell phone and thought, "I can't do that now." He then laughed and said, "The Dominican Republic. No, I said no more jungle work after I went to Venezuela. No more damn snakes."

Chapter 6

"The pipeline is flowing again"

September 11

RICK OWENS HAD SHED OVER TWENTY-FIVE POUNDS since he started jogging, and watching Aamir Jawdat for potential espionage and terrorist activities. Owens had changed his diet, concentrating on fruits, vegetables and fish, and dumping sugars, white flour, and soda pop. He had even switched from sugar-laced coffee to green tea. His concentration at work had improved, and his energy level had gone through the roof.

His wife was overjoyed with the " New Owens", and constantly told him how much she was proud of him. He was now able to run a mile in a decent time, and he looked forward to his daily workout. He relished in the idea that now he could say, "I am in really good shape. I have made some great changes in my appearance and my job performance has become much better."

He was still using the interval training approach that had allowed him to feel like an athlete again. His wife had even agreed to start working out and had enrolled in an aerobics class at their gym. The Owens family was on a health kick.

Another consistent factor in his after-work visits to the running track near their home was the ability to continue to monitor Aamir Jawdat. While many things had changed in the time since Owens had started to work out and tail Jawdat, several constants remained. The suspected spy still sported his new, shiny, blue-and-yellow striped jogging clothes and new, matching running shoes. He still went to the tall walnut tree to the right of the banked curve of the jogging track to search for his messages from his "outside employer".

Before retrieving his messages, Aamir still looked around sheepishly to make sure no one would be watching him when he reached down to pick up a medium-sized rock from the ground. He always followed the second step of the process in a consistent manner, and had his own style of picking up a piece of paper from the ground under where the rock had been located.

Jawdat would then read the note, put the paper in his pocket, and place the rock back in its original position. He would then turn and walk back to the parking lot, in the opposite direction of Rick Olson. He would log less than one-tenth of a mile on his shiny new shoes, as he always parked close to the track.

Olson always made notes on Aamir's actions, and would always continue to walk or run around the track past the tree to the parking lot to not alert the spy that his actions were being watched. Owens was building a large file on Aamit Jawdat. Each morning following the surveillance, Owens would drive to his office with a report to discuss with his deputy director, Terry Robbins.

After reaching his destination, Owens would ride the elevator up to his office floor and settle into his corner office to ready himself for his meeting with CIO deputy director Terry Robbins.

Robbins arrived early today and after some small talk they discussed the incident report.

"Terry, let's look at one of the worst spots first. The Middle East is still embroiled in the war in Syria, and the resulting migration of illegal immigrants toward Europe."

"The numbers are up because we are in the warm weather period in Europe and there is no weather danger of crossing the sea into Greece."

"Yes, that is true and there are more immigrants now than before. The political situation and war is horrible in Syria, as one can't tell who is fighting for whom. The situation still changes daily and it is hard to unravel the political relationships to determine who is actually a friend or an enemy. No one trusts anyone else. The basic mistrust in the region has been going on for centuries."

"It is still hard to determine which terrorist group is gaining or losing strength Sir."

"True. All of the countries are also dealing with related terrorist threats. Lebanon, Qatar, Egypt, Iran, Iraq, and all of the rest are in, facing, or causing potential turmoil."

"What about the other players Sir ?"

Love and Death in the Dominican Republic

"Egypt can be added to that list. There are terrorism problems and immigrants are coming from there now also."

"Who else in active in the region ?"

"Rick, the problem in the Middle East has caused a worldwide crisis, as immigrants are fleeing many countries."

"What about Russia's actions ?"

"Russia is still wielding influence. We in America suffered from weak leadership in the presidency over the last eight years. The policy in Libya caused this situation. We still find ourselves suffering from those factors."

"Is there any good news for this situation ?"

"Yes. Now Turkey has changed and is more supportive of our efforts. They have even jailed journalists who have falsely reported on the country's situation, and are now controlling the news outlets. They are now passing laws that help fight immigration into their country. Turkey itself has been the victim of several terrorist attacks. They have seen the light."

"When it hits their country many have a change in their attitude toward illegal immigration. It would be nice if the whole situation would go away but it will not. The resulting problems have changed the world."

"It is a challenge Sir."

"Let's move on to Europe. As we discussed, the illegal immigrant invasion from the Middle East has altered Europe forever. Germany is now suffering from their ill-fated decision to welcome all immigrants at the expense of their national interests."

"Yes, they were the first to do so."

Owens continued, "Yes. They needed to reboot their population as their birth rate was falling, and in a few years they would need more people to man their economy. But, the decision has been taken at the expense of their culture. Now the German people are upset, angry, and want to reverse the decisions of their leader."

"Yes. She lost the election and is out. The new man in charge will have to clean up her mess."

"True, but it will be difficult, and take time. They now face the influx of immigrants who do not want to assimilate into the German culture, and want to impose their own beliefs on the country. And, there have been incidents of lawlessness, and attacks and serial rapes by groups of migrants on German women."

"It is no wonder that the citizenry in Germany is upset."

"Yes. The country now has to deal with terrorists who want to create havoc."

"What have they done to shore up their border security and protective abilities ?"

Owens answered, "They are now using good tactics, and the German people seem to have the resolve to help address the problems. They have started to send immigrants back to Africa when they arrive by boat. They are putting a limit on the number of illegals they will now take. If the politicians will keep a stiff backbone then there will be progress. If not, then kiss Germany goodbye."

"I agree Sir"

"Germany's neighbor, Austria, is now facing problems."

"Yes, immigrants are being smuggled into the country in railroad cars. They need to get with the program or they will be overrun."

"Spain continues to face their economic and internal terrorist problems. The AIO is still operating. We know they have sent operatives to train with the TCPLM in Columbia. We also know that they are beefing up the number of their agents in order to forcibly attempt to gain independence for their members."

"What is being done in opposition to the AIO ?"

"King Alfonso IV has given his full support to fight the resistance forces. Also, the stoppage of the drug shipments from the Dominican Republic into Europe has really hurt the AIO's cash flow. They will be concentrating on that rather than stemming the immigration flow."

"King Alfonso is a good ally for America."

"Yes he is. In England, the people voted to leave the European Confederation and stand for their national unity. They have faced terrorist problems due to the changing complexion of their population. London especially has been impacted by the illegal immigration from the Middle East. They continue to be our strongest partner in Europe but they have severe problems."

"I agree Rick."

"France has been rocked with terrorist attacks. They have a severe problem on their hands. Terrorist groups have them in their sights and have threatened many more attacks."

"Sir, they have recognized that they are a target and have been forced to deal with the problem."

"Yes, with help from the world community they may be able to keep that situation under control. I hate to say this but Germany, France, England, and the rest of Europe has brought this illegal immigrant invasion upon themselves by not opposing it from the start."

"The same situation exists in Belgium. They have been hit hard in Brussels on multiple occasions. They are now taking the problem very seriously."

"Yes, they were unprepared before they were hit."

"Switzerland has yet to be affected by terrorism, but they are on the radar screen as a warning was just issued by several terrorist groups."

"They are pretty isolated."

"True, but they only have a volunteer civil defense plan, and have no military."

"They would be prime target if the country were infiltrated."

Owens continued on the European rundown. The Eastern European countries have closed down their borders, and are not allowing immigrants to enter. If they can keep out the illegals they will be okay."

Love and Death in the Dominican Republic

"They will be one of the few countries who will be. Even Greece now wants to stop the illegal flow of bodies. If it can't be done they want to leave the federation."

"Italy is now being impacted. Even Lake Como has illegals housed near the town."

"I am sure that is causing fear for the rich and famous people who live there. I believe that Italy will start refusing to accept illegal immigrants."

"Yes the rich are facing what we middle-class people face. Europe has lost it culture, and traditions."

"What about Sweden ?"

Owens answered, "They are now experiencing problems from illegals they allowed in their country. There have been many attacks o Swedish women who have been going about their everyday life."

"What about Finland and the rest of that area ?"

"It will have problems if they admit illegals. Finland has not been hurt yet."

"That area is a cold, out-of-the-way part of the world, yet they are vulnerable."

"True. Even Asia has its own problems. China is addressing an economic downturn, and is flexing its muscles in the South China Sea by building islands on top of coral reefs and claiming the area as their own, thus violating prior agreements. Japan, which is also in a bad way economically, South Korea, Viet Nam, and the Philippines are being impacted by China's actions. North Korea has now threatened use first strikes with their nukes. China has refused to allow any illegal immigrants into their country. "

"I know that China has shown a strong military presence in the area. They just sent a naval ship through Japanese waters near Okinawa, and sent fighter jets through other countries air space. They now control the South China Sea and have pushed our influence all the way back to Guam."

"Yes, we have watched them develop into a world military power. Now, they send flights of planes over Japan that have nuclear delivery abilities."

"China is not very appreciative for our efforts in helping them become accepted into the world community, the World Trade Association, and to become a trading partner with us."

"Yes, a partner who enjoys a massive trade advantage over us, as we buy all of their cheap-labor manufactured goods. We can't compete trade-wise because of their currency manipulation."

"True. Is Russia continuing to be a problem ?"

"Yes. Russia is being hurt by the crash in oil prices. They have become a stronger player in the Middle East as a result of that problem. The recent decision by the oil producing countries in the Middle East to cut production is a result of Russia's influence."

"What about Central America Rick ?"

"They are sending immigrants through Mexico to America. That could get worse."

"What is happening in the Caribbean ?"

Love and Death in the Dominican Republic

"After stopping the drug flow from Venezuela for a short period, the Columbian drugs are once again being shipped through the Dominican Republic from Venezuela. We will talk about that in a minute."

"What about Cuba ?"

"The administration opened up relations with them, and it has been a mixed bag of results. It looks like the Bertalina government will be friendlier than his predecessors, but there is still an anti-American sentiment that has been hard to overcome."

"What about South America ?"

Owens added, "Our reports show that economic problems still exist in Argentina. They are suffering from inflation. The other countries like Chile, Bolivia, Uruguay, Paraguay, and Peru have shown very little progress in climbing out of poverty. Brazil is somewhat impacted by Columbia's drug situation. Many countries are close to collapse and martial law, which would be terrible for us as their people would migrate North towards America, and cross our borders."

"What about Columbia ?"

"They have been working with us on the drug situation. We have been assisting them in their program of eradicating cocaine crops and paying the locals to grow substitute crops like bananas."

"What about the drug cartels ?"

"The Carmelo Cartel, headed by the Candy Man, Rafael Carmelo, has not been cooperating and has increased production to flood the market with cocaine, gain market share, and permanently drive their competitors out of business. The Mountain Producers Cartel, supposedly headed by Lino Pascual, has been doing the same."

"Sir, have we uncovered any new clues about who may actually head up the Mountain Producers ?"

"No. We think it is a powerful man, named Mateo Amon, the father of Harold Gatewood's love interest Sofia Amon, who died when they visited Ella Se Cayo, is still running the operation behind the scenes. We had Jack Taylor and Harold Gatewood in Venezuela trying to find out his identity. Word has it that Mateo Amon would like to kill Gatewood. "

"Has the Colombian government made any progress ?"

"Yes, they were successful. Columbia is still continuing to fight the TCPLM. They have an agreement with Venezuela to ship the cocaine from there to the Dominican Republic. The drugs are then shipped to America and Canada."

"How does that work ?"

"Venezuela is given a cut of the profits to look the other way and let the shipments go through the country."

"It is a real criminal enterprise."

"Yes. Everyone takes a cut, including the Nazoa government, the military, and the TCPLM, who even have an office in Caracas."

"Is there any way to stop or lessen the influx of drugs into America ?"

Love and Death in the Dominican Republic

Owens replied, "We are balancing our actions in Venezuela, as we have spoken on this topic before. When Gatewood's Venezuelan lover, Luisa Gaicia worked for the TCPLM she was able to feed Gatewood information on the schedules, distribution routes, and receiving areas for the drugs. We did very well in terms of stopping the flow of drugs until she went to America with Gatewood. She has been killed by one of Gatewood's groupies so the drug pipeline to the Dominican Republic is again open."

Owens continued, "We are trying to control the supply of cocaine coming into America, lessen Venezuela's assistance to terrorist groups that threaten our borders, and keep the Nazoa government in check as best as we can."

"What are the most recent reports ?"

"Sabotage in some of the cocaine fields in Columbia may keep supply down. Inflation is still at eleven hundred percent or higher in Venezuela. The country has almost tripled the money supply. The currency had to be changed by adding a zero on the bills because of the devaluation, and money needed to buy goods will not even fit into a wallet now because too many bills of worthless denominations. The situation is the same as in German Weimer government in the 1920's. Venezuelan women travel to Columbia to sell their hair for money."

"It is a terrible situation."

"It is. The people are experiencing food shortages. They have attacked supermarkets and ambushed food deliver trucks, butchered dogs, cats, and horses for food, and now are forced by the government to work in the fields a day or two a week to help fight the shortages. They now grow food in every spare patch of dirt in the cities. Many travel to Columbia to buy food. Medical supplies are almost non-existent. Sanitary conditions in the hospital are disgusting. The situation is worsening just as we feared."

"Yes Terry. We still have measures we can do, and our backup plan is in place. We have already ordered the families of our consulate employees to return to America."

"What can we try next ?"

"We plan on buying more oil from Venezuela. We will also try to hold down production here in the United States. We will work with their lenders like China to soften their credit terms or rewrite their loans. Perhaps Harold Gatewood could help, as his ex-father-in-law is Guo Gang, the leader of China."

"He married into a highly-respected family."

"Yes, he was close to the family until his wife Akemi was killed by the Yakuza crime family."

"Gatewood has gone through misery the last four years. Now his love Luisa is dead, and he is being stalker by her killer, Susana Richards."

"Yes, Ms. Richards was just placed on our most wanted list. Hopefully, Venezuela's trade partners can urge them to get the country under control."

"Sir, that goal will be hard to accomplish due to the corruption at all levels of government in their country."

"True. We will try to work with Venezuela, despite their actions and attitudes. But, we may have to support a candidate to gain office and oust Nazoa from power. We can't take military means to remove him but we can try more subtle means to achieve our mission. The Venezuelan government is already considering on trial for crimes against the country. We believe he would flee the country, like the Nazis Adolf Eichmann and Joseph Mengele did when they went to South America. Nazoa has already thrown some of his critics in jail, the same as Abraham Lincoln did in the Civil War. It looks like revolt and bloodshed may be in store for Venezuela."

"We can use humanitarian aid in the meantime."

"That is true Terry. But that action is a temporary fix to a permanent problem. We need to keep the cocaine supply entering America at its current level and not let the cartels and Venezuela flood the market. Once they drive out their competitors through cheapening the product, they would control price and supply. But, we have to be mindful not to destroy too much supply or Venezuela would lose some of the income stream, and force them into a worse financial position."

"How will we address the problem if we can't destroy some of the product ?"

"In the past America has bought drugs to learn the identity of the cartels, producers, and their shipment dates. We might have to do that again."

"That is politically risky for any administration."

Hal Graff

"True. We have several issues to juggle."

"What else are we planning to implement Sir ?"

"We are hopeful that we can find out the information about the TCPLM's drug shipments out of Venezuela. That would be a big boost for our monitoring the cocaine supply. If we can't uncover those shipment dates and times then we will have to divert more American dollars and send more covert agents to the help out the effort."

"Is Venezuela doomed Rick ?"

"Yes, unless something unseen happens to turn the situation around. Socialism has failed once again."

"They are idiots. Socialism has never worked."

"Yes, they are Terry. We need to take precautions on how to stop the cancer from spreading from Venezuela into Central America, and then into Mexico. Mexico is the last stop before our last line of defense, our borders, are compromised, and the illegals stream in and totally ruin our country."

"We have the report for Mexico here Sir. It says that the drug cartels are still out of control, and killing each other. Violence in Mexico is rampant. Murders and kidnapping are at an all-time high. The decline in oil production has caused financial problems in the country and taken the value of the peso to a dangerously low level. Illegal immigration into America has exploded to new highs, and nothing is being done to stem the tide."

"Yes. Place that at the feet of the man currently in the White House. Luckily he will be gone in a few months. He has put the country in peril to gain enough illegal alien votes to sway the next election and keep his liberal party in control. The country is in decline. They are afraid of one of our candidates for the presidency as he wants to build a wall to keep out the illegals, and tax Mexico with a tariff on cars manufactured there and sold in America."

"Yes, there will be an attempt to have every illegal alien vote. And, I am sure that there will be election fraud. We need a nationalist for president, a person, man or woman, who will stop this insanity from continuing."

"Terry, we have dead people voting multiple times, sanctuary cities that do not stop vote fraud because it costs only a few dollars for an illegal to buy fake identification cards. Sanctuary cities do not deport illegal aliens or enforce the law against them. Fake or missing registration applications that are needed for the right to vote are rampant."

"Is there a way to stop the sanctuary cities ?"

"Yes, that is easy. The law already exists that federal money can be cut off to the cities if the cities do not follow federal law. No political party can stop the law from being enforced."

"Is there enough political resolve and money to build a wall on the border of Mexico ?"

"Yes there is enough money. A tax can be placed on the money sent by workers in the United States that is sent back to Mexico to easily do that. As far as having enough political resolve to do, that depends on which political party and candidate gets elected."

Hal Graff

"We have other issues to address the many failures of the last eight years, including national health insurance failures, the climate change hoax, and the economy."

"And, the most important problem of all Terry, is illegal immigration."

"Yes Sir, it will be an important election."

"By the way Terry, do you know if Aamir Jawdat has continued his routine in passing information to the waitress at the restaurant ?"

"Yes he is. We have agents monitoring his actions, both there and at the training camp outside Washington. D.C., in Virginia. We are completing a file on him, and the entire cell. We are identifying them one by one and monitoring what they are up to. We are using HUMIT tactics. We also have secured search warrants and are ready to move when the time is right. Sir, we could hit a homerun on this investigation, if we don't wait too long to act."

"Keep me posted. We will spring the trap when the timing is right."

"I will Sir."

"Rick, we spoke about Luisa Gaicia's murder. Poor Gatewood. Trouble is his constant companion."

"It certainly is Rick."

Chapter 7

"Our home mortgage is paid off"

September 12

AAMIR JAWDAT LOOKED AT HIS WATCH. It was two thirty p.m. eastern time. He had two hours before his shift at the CIO would end. He would walk to his car, drive to the restaurant where he would sit in his favorite booth, and be waited on by his regular waitress, Duha Dua, whose name meant "morning prayer".

Dhua had noticed Aamir when he walked through the door, and had his regular order ready by the time he sat down in the booth. He had become addicted to coffee, three sugars, and cream, since he had started coming to the restaurant.

Even though he did not need to say so, Aamir asked for the daily newspaper, which Dhua immediately brought to him. Inside the folded newspaper was a note, written in his native Arabic language, which instructed him to go to his usual drop location, the park and the running track.

Aamir went to his car, grabbed a small, black, gym bag, reentered the restaurant, and changed clothes. He then proceed to start the drive to the park and walk to the drop destination, the big tree by the far banked turn on the track. The location was visible only to a person running or walking on the banked turn of the track. It was a perfect spot for passing messages as Aamir could see anyone on the track and wait until they passed to retrieve any communications and instructions.

As Jawdat, whose name meant "goodness and excellence", drove to the park, he thought about his boyhood in his native country of Syria. His thoughts were interrupted by a phone call from his wife, Bahiyya Jawdat, whose name meant "beautiful goodness". They were childhood sweethearts, and their love was true, in order only behind their love of Allah.

Bahiyya asked him if he was headed to the park. She then said, "I hope you find treasure."

Aamir laughed and said, "I will. I will be home later."

His thoughts returned to his boyhood years in Syria. His father had been a university professor, and a severe critic of the Syrian leadership. He was what Americans called a "rabble rouser", a "community organizer", who specialized in whipping the public into a total frenzy to advance the radical changes he desired for the culture and the country. The elder Jawdat's activities and outspokenness had cost him his life, as the dictatorial leadership of the country killed him to keep him silent.

Aamir's mother was also an activist, and a dissident. She was a writer for a radical magazine that promoted revamping of existing conditions in the country and the overthrow of the government. She was the second of his parents to be killed by the Syrian leadership.

Love and Death in the Dominican Republic

Aamir was the sixth of eight children, seven boys and one girl. All were educated, and all believed in the same principles as their parents.

He was educated in madrasahs, Islamic religious schools. From age six through fourteen, Aamir attended a maktab primary school that covered basic teachings of the Quran, Arabic language, ethics, and practical skills. His secondary learning was addressed to enhance a student's possible career choice. Aamir studied reading, literature, and politics.

His higher education in Syria was conducted at a madrasah school where he studied philosophy, math, and politics. He also became fluent in English.

Due to the result of global terrorism, Aamir and his now-wife Bahiyya were both vetted and granted H-1B visas to enter the United States. Soon after arriving in America, Aamir started his career with the CIO, and entered a master's program. After graduation, he then entered a doctoral program, where he majored in Arabic history and political science. His dissertation was titled Cause and Effect of the Arab Spring and It's Impact of American Middle East Foreign Policy.

He had advanced quickly at the CIO, was well-liked by his coworkers, and appeared to be a normal, well-adjusted employee, passing his lie detector tests and security checks with flying colors.

His work centered on American relations with the countries of the Middle East. He tracked movements of militant terrorist groups and individuals, terrorist sleeper cells in America, and charitable funding of terrorist organizations. He had a finger on the pulse of all terrorist activities in the United States.

He and Bahiyya both had become citizens and appeared to be loyal Americans. Little did the CIO know that both were loyal to Syria, and their religion. Aamir was a deep cover mole for the Syrians, and was feeding information to terrorist groups. He was always one step ahead of the CIO, as he had knowledge of the organization's plans.

The Middle East was a mishmash of religious beliefs, language dialects, cultural differences, numerous groups fighting under different names, and complicated allegiances.

Arabic was the official language in the twenty-two states in the Middle East that made up the Arab Cooperative Organization. The language was based on the classical method of early-century speaking, and was complicated, with many dialects, including Levantine, Mesopotamian, Kurdish, Armenian, Syrian, and Turkish.

The Arab states included Algeria, Bahrain, Comoros, Djibouti, Egypt, Iraq, Jordan, Kuwait, Lebanon, Libya, Mauritania, Morocco, Oman, Palestine, Qatar, Saudi Arabia, Somalia, Sudan, Syria, Tunisia, United Arab Emirates, and Yemen. Four other countries were supportive, unaffiliated members, including Brazil, Eritrea, India, and Venezuela.

The region had many people, a complicated religious history, and the world's leading supply of riches in the fluid that greased the world's wheels of progress, oil.

Aamir's beloved Syria, officially called the Syrian Arab Republic, was located in the Western part of Asia, along the Levant region Eastern Mediterranean Sea. Damascus, in the Southern part of the country, and Aleppo, in the Northern part, were the two largest cities in the country.

The country was influenced by multiculturalism and foreign imperialism by the Ottoman Empire and the French. The ethnic mix of people included Arabs, Greeks, Armenians, Assyrians, Kurds, Circassians, Mandeans, Salafis, and Yazidis.

Many religious groups, including Sunnis, Christians, Alawites, Druze, Mandeans, Shites, Saladis, and Yazidis, worshiped in Syria. Largest among the groups was the Sunnis, followed by the Christians.

Aamir's knowledge about the Arab Spring revolts was a centerpiece of his work for the CIO. The uprisings were an awakening call for democracy in the region against the dictatorial regimes that had ruled for many years. Syria's revolts were against the ruling dictatorship that squashed individual rights and followed a socialist, secularist, anti-Zionist ideology.

The Arab Spring rebellions had many causes, including a growing population of the under-thirty age group, high unemployment, increased retail prices, government corruption, low wages, a low standard of living, a desire by the people to take back control of their country from the ruling family.

Hal Graff

The turmoil spread from country to country, without leaders, and was spurred on by the support of the religious masques. Social media also fueled the demand for independence from the iron-fisted rulers. The people demanded democracy, free elections, economic improvement and freedom, better human rights, decent jobs, regime change, and religious tolerance.

The movement caused many changes in the Middle East. Countries made leadership changes, and many rulers were ousted. The conflicts lead to a threat to the world's oil supply, rising prices, and political conflicts between the world's two biggest superpowers, Russia and the United States.

The feckless administration in the United States had drawn a red line in the sand, and then backed off. American presidential leadership was weak and American influence and respect both had become laughing stocks in the world community. Changes needed to be made in the upcoming election as America had lost her way abroad, and domestically.

Terrorism was running rampant in the region, and in Syria, where the United Syrian Freedom Fighters, the USFF, were on the march, and soon gained control of much of the country. The assassination of the leader of Lybia, and the domino effect of revolts rushed through the region, causing infighting, wars, outside interference, and displaced citizens who had to flee to escape religious persecution, death, and poverty.

Love and Death in the Dominican Republic

A mass exodus and an immigration crisis developed. Countless waves of people spread into Europe and caused many problems, including an attack on each country's culture and national heritage. Also included in the hordes of illegals were terrorist fighters who used the exodus to enter Europe in an attempt to change it into an Islamic-controlled area.

Terrorism attacks followed in violent waves, and Europe was forever changed, while America's president refused to honor his constitutional duty to protect the borders of the country and the rights of America's citizens. He also welcomed illegal immigrants from the Middle East, without vetting them in any substantial manner.

It was unknown how many terrorists entered America. The country then started to experience increased terrorist attacks inside the country. America had also been changed forever by the Middle East problems.

The problems were a blessing for Aamir Jawdat, the deep-cover mole at the CIO. He had enjoyed access to needed information on CIO operations and activities, and was able to give that information to the USFF, and parlay his actions into a money-making endeavor for himself.

He was a paid agent for a terrorist group whose interests were in opposition to the United States. He was committing treason under the Espionage Act number 18 U.S.C. section 794 c, which carried a life in prison sentence. He was a dangerous man who was harming America, and he was a free as a bird.

Aamir Jawdat's thinking was interrupted when he saw the exit for the park. He eased his car into the parking lot, and parked in the parking space far away from the restroom facilities so as not to be seen by anyone who might walk past the car. He exited his car, and dressed in all his splendor in his new, shiny, blue-and-yellow striped jogging clothes and new, matching running shoes, he headed to his drop point to retrieve his message from the USFF.

He surveyed the landscape, and sensing it was free of anyone's ability to see his actions, he moved to the tall walnut tree to the right of the banked curve of the jogging track. Aamir again looked around to make sure no one was watching him as he reached down and to pick up a medium-sized rock from the ground. He picked up a piece of paper from the ground under where the rock had been located, read it, then put the paper in his pocket, and placed the rock back in its original position.

He then turned and walked back to the parking lot. He smiled and laughed to himself as he walked, saying, "Not a bad reward for doing something for the USFF that I would gladly do for nothing for my beloved homeland, Syria."

Little did Jawdat know the through a set of binoculars, a set of eyes belonging to the CIO agent who was tailing him had read his lips. Jack Taylor, who had saved Harold Gatewood's life several times, smiled and said, "Well, well, Mr. Jawdat, you think you have outsmarted us. Your time will soon come, and you will not be smiling or laughing when you the CIO and the American justice system doles out your punishment for your treason."

Taylor continued, "I would bet that you will meet with the waitress once again tomorrow, and receive additional details on your new plans to continue your anti-American activities. We will be right there to close the trap on you when the time is right."

Jawdat continued his walk to his car, entered, and started his drive home. He called his wife and said he was on the way back and wondered what was for dinner. She answered, and then said, "Did you find treasure at the running track Aamir ?"

"Yes. Our home mortgage is now paid off."

"Wonderful. I am proud of you for helping the USFF in their quest to spread our beliefs, and our religion, which will bring positive change in our beloved homeland, Syria. Praise Allah."

"Yes, Bahiyya my love, praise Allah."

Chapter 8

Pool and Bananas

September 13

LINO PASCUAL, THE PERCIEVED HEAD OF THE MOUNTAIN PRODUCERS CARTEL, spoke to his right-hand man, Alfonso Roderigo, about his plans for the day.

"Alfonso, I mentioned the other day that I am going to Ella Se Cayo to meet with Mateo Amon."

"Yes, I remember."

"I will be back late tonight, or by noon tomorrow, depending on Mateo's plans for me. If we have to shoot pool and then tour the banana production facilities it may be tomorrow. I will try to get out of there as soon as I can."

"I will make sure everything in the operation runs smoothly."

"I know I am leaving things in your capable hands Alfonso."

Lino entered his vehicle, turned on the cd player and started to listen to the folk rhythm beat of the music style native to the plains of Columbia and Venezuela, the joropo. Lino sang and bobbed his head to the beat of the fandango-type music, which combined African, native Columbian and Venezuelan, and European influences. It was creole music, and suited Lino's tastes perfectly.

Many thoughts ran through Pascual's head as he drove the winding, narrow roads down the mountains to the valley below. He had brought increased production and bottom-line income to the cartel operation. While he had been compensated handsomely, he did not feel he was appreciated. He had made decisions that had brought millions of extra profits to the organization.

What really bothered him was Mateo Amon's lack of recognition for his efforts. This factor, combined with a desire to head the cartel himself had fueled his disappointment, then anger with Mateo.

He knew he could run the operation better than his employer. His lack of respect for Mateo had festered, then grown into total disrespect and disdain. He was ready to oust Mateo and be the true head of the cartel. He had crafted a plan of deceit, murder, and takeover, and he was poised to implement the daring coup.

Lino did not believe that Mateo was aware of his plan, as it had been kept secret. He considered Mateo a weak man, unaware that without him, the cartel would wither away and die, or be taken over by a stronger band of drug producers. The time was near for Mateo to voluntary step aside, or forcibly be removed from power. Lino had also planned for another option, one that would separate Mateo from his earthly presence.

As he proceeded along the roads that led to Ella Se Cayo, Lino recalled his thoughts of the last time he had been summoned to Mateo's home to discuss the attack on the warehouse that destroyed millions of dollars of cocaine supply.

He closed his eyes for an instant as the thoughts overtook his concentration. He spoke to himself, "I remember that when I gave Mateo the news about the attack on the facility, and the very being of the cartel, it was met with a calm, measured reaction by the head of the organization. I knew that Mateo would then place a plan into action that would determine who was responsible, where the guilty parties could be located, and a timetable for retribution."

Lino continued recollection of the event, "I had said that I would not want to be the responsible parties for the attack, as their death would be carried out in a particularly brutal fashion. Attacking the cartel was not good for a person's health, and soon dead bodies would be turning up. The cartel's message would be clear, do not mess with us or you will pay in a horrific way."

Despite his disdain for Mateo Amon, he was still a dangerous man when he mustered up the energy to be so.

As he approached Ella Se Cayo, a city on the Venezuelan border with Columbia, Lino knew the routine he would face when he reached Amon estate. He would walk to the front door, be met by the butler, and ushered to a sitting room to wait for Mateo. He dreaded what would then once again follow.

Mateo Amon would welcome him, they would sit and visit for a short time in the sitting room, then Mateo would take him a nearby room to play pool, a game in which Lino did not excel, and hated. After some discussion on the state of the cartel and the discussion of any recent problems, Mateo would show Lino his banana operation. He would be required to visit the growing areas, and the factory. The tour would be torture for him, as his host would be very talkative about the business he loved so much. He was wild about the banana business, a condition that Lino considered borderline psychotic.

During the tour Lino would hear the story about the Amon family's big party for many of the local dignitaries every year. It is a costume party. Mateo would describe how he always dressed as a banana. He would always say how his costume would cause so much embarrassment for his wife. But, after all of these years, he knew not to try to change the conversation when it came time for Mateo to discuss his love of the banana business.

Pascual turned off his vehicle engine and walked to the front door. He was met the butler who, as expected, led him to a sitting room to wait for his employer. His wait was a short one, as Mateo Amon, and his wife, greeted him.

As they shook hands, Pascual thought about the Amon's background.

Both were from a small town in Columbia, ten miles from the Venezuelan border. Lino did not know why, but that fact stuck in his memory. The couple had married young, and moved to Venezuela when Mateo Amon had started law school in Ella Se Cayo. After law school he started his law practice in the town, quickly invested in banana farms, then moved into the banana processing business. The Amon efforts were an outstanding example of people's ability to start from nothing and build success upon success.

Mateo Amon was an educated and successful man, a lawyer and a businessman, cultured, refined, and gentlemanly. He had been a ruggedly handsome man, and had enjoyed an air of confidence. Pascual was shocked to see how Mateo had aged since his last visit.

His hair, eyebrows, and mustache were now gray, no doubt from the stress of their daughter Sofia's death while hiking with her lover Harold Gatewood, the American baseball player who had become a persistent thorn in the side of all of the cartels in Columbia.

Mrs. Amon had been a pretty and outgoing woman. She also was educated, successful, cultured, and very loving. She was an artist, and had always been dressed in a white painter's smock, adorned with many paint smudges in the bright blue, red, white, gold, and green colors she used in her craft, when they had previously met.

She also had aged, as her hair had turned white. She had lost weight and looked skeleton-thin, and her radiant smile had transformed into downturned wrinkles near the corners of her mouth. She was suffering from the same malady as her husband, the grief of losing their daughter Sofia.

Grief was not first-time visitor to the Amon family. They had lost four unborn children due to miscarriages, prior to Sofia's birth. She was a gift from heaven and had been spoiled since birth. When Lino mentioned that he was hopeful the couple was making progress adjusting to the loss of Sofia, Mrs. Amon's facial expression changed, as she beamed with pride at the mention of her daughter's name.

The Amon's were one of the richest, most successful, well-respected families in Venezuela, but like all families, they could not escape God's plan. Unfortunately, Sofia's death was part of the Amon story, and the couple was learning to live with the tragedy. Despite what Lino had planned for Mateo he did feel sorry for the couple's loss.

After Mrs. Amon excused herself in order to continue her painting, the men sat down in the chairs in the sitting room and started to speak.

"Thank you for coming here today Lino."

"I am always at your service Sir."

"I always appreciate your excellent work Lino."

"Thank you Sir."

"Before we talk about the cartel business I want to ask you if you are happy with your position at the cartel."

"Yes Sir, I am. You have been very gracious and supportive of my efforts. I appreciate that very much."

"Good. You know that I expect, and reward, loyalty."

"Yes Sir. You know I am loyal."

"I do. You have run the cartel in an excellent manner."

Hal Graff

"Thank you."

"I hope you are enjoying your life and are able to do what pleases you when you are not at the production facility or the headquarters in the mountains."

"I am Sir. I thank you for letting me have enough vacation to get away."

"How is Alfonso Roderigo performing in your absence ?"

"He is doing well. He knows the business and is aware of what you expect of me. In turn, he knows what I expect of him in order to make sure the cartel succeeds."

"Very good work. You have done a good job of mentoring his progress."

"Thank you Sir."

"Lino, I want to talk to you about the supply problems, the shipments into the Dominican Republic, and the problems in the Venezuelan government. Let's shoot some pool while we discuss those matters."

"Yes Sir, I would enjoy that."

As the two men headed to the pool room, Lino Pascual said to himself, "I was hoping to avoid this torture. Oh how I hate to play pool."

As the men chalked up their pool cues, Mateo Amon spoke, "Please tell me about the supply problem."

"The distribution supply routes were compromised when a worker in the Caracas office of the TCPLM gave the information to her lover, Harold Gatewood, who then gave the specific details to the CIO. As such, they knew when and where our shipments were to be made in the routes through Central America to Mexico to the Southwestern United States, and the flights into the Dominican Republic."

"Did you say Harold Gatewood ?"

"Yes. I am sorry to have to mention his name Sir, as I know he was responsible for your daughter Sofia's death. I must apologize as I know that information causes you grief."

"Do not worry about it. I need to know that and I am glad you told me."

"Thank you Sir."

"What is the status of the Venezuelan national government ?"

"The country is in shambles. The oil price has started to go up as the oil producing countries in the Middle East have agreed to cut production, which will cause a shortage and drive prices back up."

"Good."

"The citizens are in panic. There are shortages in food and medicine. The military is profiting by selling these two items on the black market. And, many people are fleeing the country to find food, medicine, jobs, and hope for the future."

"What about President Nazoa ?"

"He has survived a recall election attempt and will probably not be impeached. He will stay in office, but no one knows for how long. He has raised the minimum wage six times to help the people fight inflation."

"What is the outlook ?"

Hal Graff

"It looks bleak for him, and for the country. There are so many problems."

"What plans have you started to bribe and control his possible successor ?"

"Our contacts inside the government have identified the two people who might succeed Nazoa. We are building a file, and checking on their vices to see if we can control him through blackmail."

"Please send me that information."

"I will."

"What are you doing in the Caribbean ?"

"We are back in business and the TCPLM has set up new delivery routes and drop points inside the country."

"Are we distributing the necessary bribe money to the Dominican Republic president and politicians ?"

"Yes Sir. We are currently paying him within the budgeted payment range."

"Good work."

"How soon before we are back to our one hundred percent figure for total shipments ?"

"We are currently at seventy-five percent. We should be at the one hundred percent in another month."

"Are they any obstacles that will delay that effort ?"

"Not at this time."

"Do you think there is a scenario that might again develop into a problem for our deliveries and cash flows ?"

"As usual, it would come from the Americans if there is to be one."

Love and Death in the Dominican Republic

"Are there any CIO agents operating in the Dominican Republic now ?"

"None that are known of Sir."

"Very well Lino. Please monitor the American CIO presence in the Dominican Republic and let me know of any possible changes."

"I will Sir."

"Lino you need to work on your pool game."

"I am not in your league."

"Practice is the key."

Thankfully, Lino thought the pool torture had ended.

"Lino, we are now going to tour the banana plant. While we do I want to talk to you about Harold Gatewood."

Pascual's heart sank, as he was now going to be subjected to another banana plant tour. Mateo and Lino headed to the banana fields. Mateo conducted a seminar on the preference for deep, well-drained soil needed to grow a quality crop. He said that the climate in Columbia, where his banana crop was located, was ideal. He discussed his growth from a banana farmer to a banana processor and shipper. After touring the fields he shuttled Lino to his banana factory.

Mateo discussed the steps in the overall banana sales process. Fields used to grow bananas then needed to be harvested by picking the crop, and transporting it to the packing shed to hang and dry. At the next stage of the process larger bundles needed to be divided into more store-friendly bunches. The bananas next needed to be washed, dried, refrigerated, sorted by quality, labeled, shipped, and marketed world-wide.

Market research, machinery purchases and updates, and fertilizer management were also involved. Tractors, washing tanks, storage buildings, boxes, shipping docks, offices, and other equipment were needed. Mateo's company grew premium quality bananas that demanded a quality price.

He believed in taking good care of his employees with the best machinery, safety measures, and benefits in the industry. He was possessed by the banana business, and Lino, his mind now a conglomeration of mush, was glad to get back to the house so he could thank his employer and return to his vehicle for his escape from pool, the banana business, and start the ride back to the cartel headquarters in the mountains.

As he drove along the route home, he said to himself, "He is even more frail, weak, grief-stricken, and senile than he was on my last visit. It is time for me to take him out and gain control of the cartel."

Mateo Amon had waved goodbye, walked to his office, dialed a number of a contractor he had heard about from his good friend and business associate, Damon Justice from America.

"Hello'"

"Hello. Can this call be traced ?", asked Amon.

"No I use throw-away cell phones."

"My research tells me you perform a service I would like carried out."

"What kind of service ?"

Love and Death in the Dominican Republic

"Removal of an overly-ambitious employee."

"Is the package returnable or to be permanently removed ?"

"Permanently removed."

"By what means ?"

"Any, just so it is done."

"How many units are in the package ?"

"One."

"The head of a country ?"

"No."

"With nuts or without ?"

"With."

"In what area of the world is this package located ?"

"It is located in the mountains of Columbia."

"Would the disposal service need to be done in public ?"

"No,"

"Is the package heavily guarded ?"

"No but he is a dangerous man in his own right."

"Are you worried about collateral damage to other packages ?"

"No."

"Payment for disposal fees are based on many factors. The location is remote Sir. The package would know his environment and I would not so the fee will be higher."

"I understand."

"One other thing, dangers encountered in disposal, my exit after disposal, and quick access to another location."

Hal Graff

"Ok. Go on please."

"The more severe the dangers the higher the disposal fee. So the fee charged will also take those factors into consideration."

Amon answered, "Understood."

"When is the disposal date for the package ?"

"As soon as possible."

"Is the disposal for an aware or unsuspecting package ?"

"Unsuspecting."

"Have you contacted other package disposal firms ?"

Amon proudly stated, "No. I only purchase services from the world's best vendors."

"Will you be near the package disposal location ?"

"No."

"We guarantee total package disposal."

"Excellent."

"Disposal fees vary."

"I understand. What is the range ?"

"It will cost one million dollars for total package disposal in a location such as mentioned."

"It seems a little high."

"Top of the line, world-class work demands an appropriate price."

"Alright"

"The disposal location must be known so disposal routes and times can be arranged."

"How much planning is involved in this type of package disposal ?"

Love and Death in the Dominican Republic

"Based on the location and escape risks of this disposal, six weeks from the delivery and receipt of the first half of the fee."

"What about last minute changes ?"

"Small changes in the disposal are not a problem in either cost or service areas."

"How are payments for disposal handled ?"

"You will send it by wire to a numbered account. You will pay half down and half upon disposal of the package."

"Did you ever have a client who did not pay your fees ?"

"None that are alive now to tell about it", replied the assassin.

"I want the package disposal service."

"Do you have any questions ?"

"Yes."

"Go ahead please."

"How long have you been in the disposal business ?", asked Amon.

"Over thirty years."

"Is your service totally confidential ?"

"Yes."

"That is a must for my needs. It must be adhered to at all times. Otherwise, I will not utilize your services."

"Of course, I understand. For both the client, and the firm, confidentiality is completely guaranteed."

"If events change and the package removal is not desired any more, then there is no charge ?"

Hal Graff

"The charge would be for any expenses incurred, and half of the total fee. No work would be done prior to entering into an agreement for disposal services of the package."

"Okay. I want the service performed. Where do I wire the first payment ?"

After the discussion of the details of the payment transaction and other details related to the contract-for-hire killing, Mateo Amon said, "There is one more thing. I will want you to perform a second contract for me once this first one is completed."

"Do you know the details of that contract need ?"

"Not at this time."

"Then we will conclude our first contract, and I will then be happy to work with you again on your second contractual need."

Mateo Amon thanked his new contract-for-hire assassin, and smiled. He would finally get to the man who was responsible for the death of his beautiful daughter Sophia. Harold Gatewood would soon get what was coming to him.

Chapter 9

Icterus, Icterus

September 14

PRESIDENT NAZOA WALKED TO HIS OFFICE WINDOW, looked into the beautiful courtyard, and smiled. His actions were relaxing and satisfying distractions he performed many times during his daily routine. He looked out his office window at the beautiful trees adorned in their cloak of leaves. His favorite companions, the birds, were still chirping and enjoying their lives, and flittering from tree to tree.

Nazoa again thought that if he were a bird he would fly far away, to a place where he could be happy. Conditions in the country had reached a tipping point. If he were forced from office he would try to go to a country that would give him asylum. The Nazis had lived in Argentina and Brazil after escaping. He had stolen more money from the country than a person could possibly spend in a lifetime. He would use that money to buy his freedom.

The fifty-eight year old, short, five foot-six inch, mustachioed, dark haired, pock- marked faced man moved from the window to the area behind his ornate teak wood desk and gazed at the pictures on the office wall that detailed his rise to power. A picture of his early days in the military captured the determination and ruthlessness that had led him on his rise to high rank and into politics. It also showed his former thin, svelte figure, which had surrendered to a habit of overeating, drinking, and smoking fine cigars. The habit had presented him an annoying, ever-present cough.

He wondered why the years of his life had passed so quickly. It seemed like yesterday when he remembered his military career in the jungle, and his first entry into the drug trade. While he was not a user himself, he had seen the effects of the drug on many people. The white powder was only a vehicle which had led to his association with his predecessor, and his climb to high government office.

There had been casualties due to his brutal rise to power. The murder of his comrades and his country's citizens, and drug-related deaths of thousands of users in other countries around the world were three results. He had pulled the trigger in some of the cases. He was indirectly responsible for the drug deaths on far away foreign soil.

Some of the addicted users had died quickly, and some had fought the battle to the end. But, the result was the same as if he had killed them himself. He had grown numb to what he had done, and long ago had stopped viewing the consequences of his actions. He did not care, and the deaths were meaningless to him, as power had rotted his morality.

He had come to office due to the death of his mentor, from whom he inherited his current situation in the government. He had been left a powder keg of brewing problems, and a host of nefarious individuals with whom he had to monitor. It was a tough job that required a merciless strongman, a position for which he had been born to fill.

Venezuelan President Ramon Nazoa rose from his desk, again walked to the window, and saw two men exit a white, four-door government car in front of the palace. A tall, thin, black-haired man, holding a satchel full of important papers, closed the front passenger-side door of the vehicle, removed his glasses, and cleaned them with the white handkerchief he had removed from his right back pocket. Nazoa laughed at the man's actions, as it was typical for an accountant.

Juan Emilio, his loyal friend, had been sent to Venezuela from Madrid, Spain by the Basque AIO terrorist organization. His job was to work with the government in the areas of terrorist training and the drug distribution. He was detail-oriented and had developed into a valued member of the Venezuelan government's cabinet.

The second man, sporting black hair and mustache, a trim build, and dressed in the typical military khaki-colored uniform, exited the driver's side of the vehicle. He stretched his arms toward the bright overhead sun, straightened his brown tie, and walked around the front of the car. He spoke to Emilio, and motioned for him to start the walk to the palace.

Johan Diaz was the second most powerful man in the government, and Nazoa's trusted ally. Today, he

Hal Graff

and Emilio would be assisting the president in a discussion about the problems the country faced, and their own political futures.

Still gazing out the window, Nazoa waited for the two men to make the trek to his office. He watched the birds in the courtyard. He admired how they flittered from tree to tree, seemingly without a care in the world. He longed for his lost youth when he too was happy, carefree, and not cursed with the burdens of running a country that had recently exploded and had been ripped apart at the seams by economic, financial, and social problems.

After Emilio and Diaz's arrival, Nazoa welcomed them and asked them to sit down.

"Welcome comrades."

Both men replied that they were happy to be there, and that they had brought the requested reports.

"Gentlemen, we will start our talks today with an update on drug trade. We will cover the recent developments in the cocaine distribution chain and the political events in North America, Europe, and the Caribbean."

Johan Diaz asked, "Sir, will we also discuss the potential political problems in our own country ?"

"Yes. We need to plan for our own safety and future careers."

"Thank you. We wanted to discuss that situation also."

Nazoa outlined the drug trade shipment situation. "As you both know we have suffered a serious setback in the shipping of our drug shipments due to the leak in the Caracas office of the TCPLM. I have been assured that the leakage has now been stopped with the death of the employee, Luisa Gaicia. The TCPLM has reestablished safe shipping procedures. They have set up new drop points for receiving shipments in the Dominican republic, and have changed departure locations and shipping schedules."

Diaz asked, "Is it correct that Luisa Gaicia was killed in America, where she fled with her lover, Harold Gatewood ?"

"Yes, that is correct. The good news is that we are back on schedule and shipments are flowing in and out of the Dominican Republic on a regular basis."

Both Emilio and Diaz were pleased, saying, "Our cash flow is again back to normal. We will now have enough money to start paying the military for their help in making the drug shipments possible."

"Yes, that is correct. We have been able to prevent a military coup, and now do not face a takeover caused by the inability to pay hush money. Also, the cartels are now also relieved that the money flow has been reestablished. They are no longer a threat to help remove us from office. We are partners once again."

Emilio asked, "What other good news is there ?"

"Somehow, we have avoided a recall election, and have mustered enough political votes through intimidation and blackmail, and bribery to fend off an impeachment vote."

"Our fortunes have trended up Sir."

Hal Graff

"Yes, so far. I have also tried to pacify the citizens by raising the minimum wage six times to keep up with the crippling rate of inflation, which was nine hundred percent last year."

Diaz asked, "What can we do to survive a rate of increase like that ?"

"It is a mess. The GDP has also fallen by twenty percent in the last year. We are hopeful that the recent agreement by the oil producing countries in the Middle East will cause a supply shortage and drive up prices to the level where income will again start to flow into the government coffers."

"We hope that is a reality Sir. What are we going to do about the problems that remain ?"

"The shortages in food and medicine have caused riots. We ordered the military to handle food and medicine distribution. That led to black market sales of those supplies, which brought money into the government and pacified the military. But the problems are still present. People are fleeing to Brazil and Columbia for those items."

"Yes Sir. We also know that the people are eating horsemeat, birds, dogs, and breaking into the zoo to kill the animals for food."

"You are correct Johan. That situation is still a problem. The people want those commodities and a decent job to make enough money to survive."

"Sir, do we know how many people have fled the country ?"

Love and Death in the Dominican Republic

"Hundreds of thousands have left Venezuela. A silver lining in the situation is that those people are not here to cause problems. We will try to control the others with an iron-fisted approach and keep a lid on the situation. So far we have been able to do so."

"We have lost face in the world, and our citizens have lost faith in us. We are now seen as the latest failed socialist country. In particular, America is crowing about socialism's failure. The Americans are so stupid. They have had a bigger socialist in office the last eight years than we are. He has ruined their economy and worldwide reputation. They will be in our shoes soon."

"Sir, how can we get our supportive partners like Cuba and China to help us ?"

"Cuba is still trading with us and sending medical care to ease that problem. China has addressed our trade terms and has reduced the rate we are paying, which has been helpful. As we discussed before, if the Middle Eastern countries hold the line on oil production it will send dollars into our treasury. That action alone will ease much of the tension."

"Can Brazil and Columbia help us ?"

"Brazil is being overrun with the migration of our people into their country. They are disgusted with us, but they are providing some degree of help."

"What about the Columbian government ?"

"They are very angry that we are sending a constant flow of our citizens into their country. They try to encourage those illegal immigrants to pass on through

Columbia and into Central America, Mexico, and then into America. They don't want to help us. The most important help from Columbia will come from our partners, the drug cartels, as their product will lead to our share of the drug market profits."

"Sir, is there anything else we can try ?"

"We are facing inflation, depression, and a geopolitical shift in our region and the world. Our main commodity needs to rebound, but we are just one spoke in that wheel. The overall oil market is depressed and underpriced. Populations are on the move and they are heading to economically sound countries to escape poverty caused by wars and economic failures such as ours."

"It sounds dismal Sir."

"In reality it is my friends."

"What are your plans Sir ?"

"I will try to help the country as long as I can. But, the time will come that we three will be forced to flee Venezuela. The key is leave with our heads till attached to our bodies."

"We both think along the same lines Sir."

"You should stick it out with me as long as you can. I would suggest we all depart at the same time, unless you have an escape plan now."

"We are grateful that you have allowed us to make enough money to have that option Sir."

"You are both talented and will be in demand by countries such as ours and by organizations such as those that we deal with. Obviously, you will need to find a safe haven where you will be free from extradition back to Venezuela to face prison, or worse."

"Do you have any suggestions ?"

"Our friends in Lebanon would be receptive, as would some countries in South America. Your choice would be dependent upon the current political environment in the various countries. If you have enough money you can hide out for many years in an unknown island location."

"Thank you Sir. We will remain loyal to you, and will not leave until you suggest we do."

"I appreciate your loyalty. We must see what will unfold in the future. We are still in control here. If we make the right moves, and the economic possibilities break in our favor we still may be able to stay in Venezuela. But, we do need to make contingency plans should we be required to bolt in order to save our necks."

"Thank you for the advice Sir."

Nazoa bid Emilio and Diaz goodbye, and then walked to his office window. He watched his friends, the birds, fly and hop from branch to branch. He was in awe of their quick movements, and their sure footing. He envied their life.

He then thought about his happiest time in life, his boyhood. In all probability, he would soon need to fly like the birds to his new safe location where he would hope to lead a relaxed life away from all of the problems he now faced.

Hal Graff

He looked at the tree closet to the window and spied an Icterus Icterus, the troupial, Venezuela's national bird. The beautiful bird had a dark black head and beak, dark black and white wings, and a bright orange body. The gorgeous bird made eye contact with President Nazoa. The president took the opportunity to ask it a question.

"Should I fly away now or stick it out in the country a while longer ?"

The bird did not chirp or sing an answer. It merely looked at the president and then flew away.

Chapter 10

"You're in demand"

September 15

WHACK ! WHACK ! THE SOUND OF Gatewood's bat slamming into the baseball as it rested on the batting tee was loud and authoritative. While his body was healing well and his strength was coming back, Gatewood did not want to overdo his workouts in fear of placing too much stress on his muscles. The last thing he wanted to happen was to suffer a relapse.

Prior to hitting off a tee Harold had done his tai chi, taekwondo, meditation, and stretching exercises. His body was heading toward readiness and his mind was clear. He knew he could come back as good as or better than before.

After finishing his workout and heading to the house Harold answered a phone call.

"Hello."

"Hi Harold. This is Randle Quinn."

"Good morning Randle."

"How are your workouts coming along ?"

"I am making nice steps forward."

"I wanted to let you know that I am getting several calls from people who want your services."

"What are they ?"

Hal Graff

"The scouting organization still wants you to go to the Dominican Republic. They have upped the amount they will pay you."

"I am not interested."

"Okay. I also got a call about you managing."

"Where ?"

"In the Idaho / Washington League."

"What teams are in the league ?"

"It is a Rookie League classification. It has a short season. They travel by bus."

"There are twelve teams. The North division includes the teams in Washington. They are the Allison Ambassadors, Moose Ear Trappers, Knight Owls, Sunset Hawks, Richards Ramblers, and the Fall River Ducks."

"What are the teams in Idaho ?"

"They are the Acton Anvils, Branson Bison, Elliott City Eagles, Foosland Fighting Falcons, Granite Mountain Greyhounds, and the team that wants you, South Gibson Giants."

"The South Gibson Giants ?"

"Yes. All of the towns are small, from four thousand to eight thousand population."

"Where is South Gibson ?"

"It is up North, near the Washington state line. It is close to Trout Lake."

"I have heard of the lake. They have a special strain of rainbow trout that grows very big. There is also a river that leads into the lake that has great fishing."

Love and Death in the Dominican Republic

"Is there a lake in the world that you don't know about Harold ?"

Gatewood laughed and said, "Maybe there is one somewhere."

"Harold the money is not great but you would be getting managerial experience."

"I am not ready for that yet Randle."

"There is one more option. "

"Pat Sullivan wants you to join him in Miami, with the Raiders. You can be a coach on the big league team, a special-assignment scout, manage in the minor leagues, or work on the general manager's staff in the front office."

Harold thought about Pat Sullivan's offer. It was a good one. But the idea of living near Islamorada, Florida haunted him. Harold gazed out over the corn field behind his house and thought about the events in Islamorada, where his love Yeong Hyeon was killed by the tiger shark when they did a shallow-water scuba diving outing.

Harold remembered the details of the tragedy as if it were yesterday. The divers had entered the water from the flat platform at the back of the boat. The vessel's layout was very handy for the diver's entry to and exit from the water. The ship's dive crew had assisted the divers off and on to the platform. The trip was a two-tank dive so the couple would have plenty of time to enjoy their surroundings and be together. Just before the first tank ran out of air, they had surfaced and strapped on another tank.

Hal Graff

Afterwards, Yeong entered the water first, waited for Harold, and then they both descended and had inspected the coral and small fish in the area. They had stayed close together for a few minutes until she started to lose her concentration. The distance between them was grew rapidly, and Harold had become concerned as she wandered out into deeper water at the far end of the submerged reef.

He had motioned to her to swim near him. She had shrugged her shoulders, signaling she did not understand his message. She continued to drift away. She became caught in an undertow and did not realize it. Harold had swam furiously toward her, finally reaching her and started to help her swim back closer to the boat, and away from the reef's deeper shelf.

Finally she made it back to the original area nearer the boat. She had turned to look at Harold and her eyes suddenly grew large. Above and behind Harold, a large shark, sixteen or seventeen feet long, had noticed his presence, and was scrutinizing his shape, and air bubbles. Yeong had frantically waved at Gatewood to get his attention. She had pointed up, urging him to check out the water column above him, where the shark was circling. After doing so Harold started to swim toward Yeong and the boat.

The large shark, a tiger, blessed with blue-green skin and a white underbelly, and cursed with a voracious appetite, and a long record of human attacks, had circled above Harold as he swam toward freedom. Yoeng also swam as fast as she could and had reached the boat. Before she surfaced she had waved and encouraged Gatewood to swim faster as the shark was getting closer.

She had then ascended to the back platform of the boat and was lifted up, free of and safe from the killer below. After removing her tank she had peered down into the water to check Harold's progress. He was still swimming as fast as he could but the large predator was gaining on him. Tigers were slow swimmers, but were strong enough to use a burst of speed to capture their prey at the last minute before it could escape.

As the shark closed the distance on Harold, Yeong had started to yell. "Harold hurry. Hurry. Swim as fast as you can darling."

The boat's captain and his first mate had also started to yell to Gatewood, telling him to swim faster. Harold then surfaced, grabbed the platform, and started to pull himself up. The two boatmen had grabbed his arm and started to jerk him on to the platform when the tiger shark raised its head out of the water in an attempt to clamp its sharp teeth and huge mouth on Gatewood's legs.

Yoeng had screamed as the shark's huge mouth missed most of Harold's legs. Only the outside row of the shark's teeth had found flesh, slicing into the swimmer's right leg. As blood flowed from the wound into the water, Harold, in pain, had dropped back into the water and the tiger had circled for another bite. Yeong had moved closer to the two boatmen to hopefully help Harold out of the water.

Hal Graff

The tiger had completed his circle and swam in a direct line toward Harold. All three of the people standing on the back of the boat had yelled for Harold to swim to the platform and grab their hands so they could help him. As Yoeng had moved closer to help, the first mate had moved to his right, knocking her off balance, and causing her to fall overboard. Now there were two people in the water, both potential targets for the huge shark.

The shark then again moved toward the boat, somewhat confused by both people being overboard. The shark's indecision allowed Yeong to swim back to the boat, where she had been pulled to the safety of the platform as the shark swam by her. Gatewood was then able to gain his composure and had started to get close to the platform. The shark was gaining quickly on Harold. The tiger had again raised its head to snap down on Harold's body, which was now half way up on the platform. Yeong had stepped closer and reached for Harold's arm.

The tiger had clamped down and found flesh and bone. Harold had rolled over on the platform, disoriented and in pain. He had escaped. The tiger had grabbed Yeong's outstretched arm, biting it off at the elbow, and had pulled her into the water. Yeong went under the surface of the water, then resurfaced, bleeding and disoriented. She had bobbed in the water like a cork, as the shark circled for another pass at her in the water.

The tiger had then headed below the surface and disappeared. Yeong had tried to swim to the platform but could not accomplish the task due to her missing arm. She dog-paddled as best as she could, but had to keep her head above the water level to see where she needed to go. The shark had suddenly raised it head, after swimming close to Yeong, and clamped its jaws down on her neck. The shark then shook her like a rag doll, and then both disappeared under the water. Mercifully, Gatewood, in pain and disoriented on the platform, had not seen the grisly event.

The shark had then surfaced far from the boat, and Yeong's headless body had floated to the surface. The Tiger circled then time and time again, each time, biting off chunks of Yeong's lifeless body. Gatewood had passed out. The two boatmen had then hoisted him into the bottom of the boat, cranked up the twin inboard motors, and sped to shore. He had been rushed to the hospital where the doctors used one hundred fifty-four stitches to close his wounds. He was then sedated and slept through the night. Upon awakening he asked, "Where is Yeong ?"

The doctor had then told him that she was gone.

Harold was completely lost in the memories of Yeong's death, and continued to gaze at the cornfield.

Randle Quinn finally spoke, "Harold, are you still there?"

"Yes."

"Are you alright ?"

Hal Graff

"Yes. I was thinking about Yeong's death. I don't know if I want to live near Islamorada. The memories are too haunting."

"I understand. Do you want me to tell that to Pat Sullivan ?"

"No. Just tell him that I appreciate everything but that I need more time."

Harold, knew that Pat Sullivan would reply, "Time for what ?"

Gatewood then spoke, "Randle, please tell him I just need more time, and that I will be open to working with him once when I am through these personal tragedies that continue to haunt me. I know he will understand."

"I will tell him what you said. I will also tell him that you appreciate his confidence in you, and that you would like to keep the door open to work with them in the future."

"That sounds good. Thanks."

"Are you sure you are alright ?"

"I don't know Randle. I may not be ready for anything right now. You know I want to come back as a player."

"I know."

"Are you positive that you want me to tell all of these people you are not interested now ? Harold, maybe you need something to do to take your mind off of your troubles. Getting back to work might do you some good."

"I know. That is good advice. But, I am working on my comeback as a player. I want to keep that secret."

"Alright."

"Tell them that I need time to myself right now due to Luisa's death, and that I will be receptive to offers in the future."

"I will be here for you if you need anything Harold."

"Thanks Randle."

Gatewood placed his cell phone down on the kitchen table, and refocused his gaze on the cornfield. He knew he still had the desire and the passion to make another comeback.

He smiled and thought, "I want to make it back to the big leagues, even if it is for one more season. That would give me more than ten years of service. With all of the injuries that I have suffered, ten years would be very gratifying."

He then poured himself a glass of cold water and continued his thoughts. "Truthfully, I would settle for one more at-bat. Just to be in uniform, to smell the outfield grass, rub the dirt near home plate on my hands, take batting and infield practice, and listen to my name and number announced as I walk to home plate to hit would be an honor. One more at-bat would satisfy me."

Harold became quiet and looked at the cornfield again. After a moment, he said, "Just one more at-bat would be a rewarding. I love baseball."

Hal Graff

Chapter 11

Rough Sledding

September 16

LEAL SERVIDOR HAD ASCENDED to the Mexican presidency when his predecessor, Alto Roble, apparently died in a murder-suicide with two female companions aboard his yacht. The fallout from the event was massive as the ugliness of Roble's lifestyle of drugs and philandering made it to the front pages of the world's newspapers. Scandal and embarrassment became Roble's legacy and Mexico's shame.

The Robe situation had made Servidor's transition into Mexico's leadership position difficult. The difference in Roble's lifestyle and his own could not have been clearer. Personally, he had nothing in common with Roble. Frankly, he despised the man because of his conduct, lack of morals, and his absence of a belief in God.

Leal was a devoted family man, had married his grade school sweetheart, was active in his church, and had lived his life in an honorable manner. He had entered politics at the local level, winning a seat on the school board, and then being elected mayor of his small home town in the most Northwestern state of Mexico.

Love and Death in the Dominican Republic

He won his first term in the Chamber of Disputes, the Camara de Diputados, at age twenty-six. He soon won the respect of his peers and was elected speaker of body at age thirty.

His choice as vice-president was done in an attempt to take the pressure off of Roble's pattern of corruption, personal habits, his ties to the drug cartels, and his antagonistic attitude toward Mexico's biggest trade partner, the United States.

Servidor hated the drug cartels. He had lost his younger brother to drugs provided by the cartel owned by Slavado Masas, the El Avispon Picante, the "stinging hornet". His father had been a businessman, operating a feed and hardware store. The elder Servidor had been forced to pay protection money to the Masas cartel. His mother had worked at the local library. Both were now deceased. Leal had come from good stock.

Servidor sat in his office and thought about how he had been chosen to become the vice-president. He had been as surprised as everyone else when he had been picked out of the blue for the position. His being on the ticket was a counterbalance and a breath of fresh air to the poisoned atmosphere of the Roble administration.

Leal had sent a note of condolences to Harold Gatewood when Luisa had been killed. He now felt that enough time had passed for Gatewood to deal with the grief of her passing, and called him at his cell number.

"Hello, his is Harold Gatewood."

Hal Graff

"Harold, this is Leal Servidor."

"Hello. It is nice to hear from you. How are you ?"

"I am fine. Actually, I am calling to see how you are doing."

"Thank you. I am making progress."

"I wanted to call and tell you how sorry my family and I are about Luisa's death."

"Thank you."

"We all loved her. She was a kind, loving soul. My children miss her terribly. She was so wonderful with them."

Harold said, "Thank you. She brought sunshine into everyone's lives."

"My children have had a hard time adjusting to her passing."

"I hope they are doing better."

"Thank you. We explain to them that Luisa is in heaven and smiling on them."

"Luisa told me how grateful she had been for you hiring her as the children's nanny. She said that she loved you all very much. She had cried when she had to leave them when we flew back to America."

"Thank you. She was very special and quickly became part of our family."

"Yes she was. How are you doing Leal ?"

"The transition has been rough sledding. I have been surprised by the scope of my new position. It looks much easier from the outside than what it is once a person has the job. There is much more to it but once you focus and prioritize what is needed it becomes manageable."

"You will do well because you are a good man."

"Thank you Harold. You are a good man also. You have done much to help Mexico by helping bring focus on Roble and the cartels."

"Thank you. We Americans are thankful you are now in office as our countries can now work together much more effectively. We all look forward to working with you."

"Thank you. We all need to put aside past differences and work on the areas where we can make progress. We need to stop the march of illegal immigrants flowing through Mexico on their way to America. We also need to stop the inflow of drugs from the cartels to the United States. Once we control those two issues we can work on a new trade agreement."

"Leal, what is happening with the "Stinging Hornet" ?

"He is still a big problem. He is opposing my reform measures whenever he can."

"Please be careful. We both know he is very dangerous."

"I will. Harold, that advice applies to you too. The hornet has it in for you too as he considers you one of the reasons that Alto Roble is dead. He wants to even the score with you for negatively impacting his business and the flow of drugs through his cartel. He also blames you for losing a close friend, and a protective shield in the Mexican government."

"Thanks for the heads up about him. I know he hates me for several reasons. I want you to know that I have the same feelings for him. I consider him an evil man who has no heart, character, or soul. The world will be a better place when he no longer walks upon it."

"I agree Harold. He is human debris."

"When are you coming to America to go to a baseball game ?"

"I want to come when you make your comeback."

"I want that to happen, and for you to be in the row by the dugout. I will make all of the arrangements for you and your family to be my guests. But, first I have to work hard and make my way back. I know what you mean about tough sledding. Making comebacks are hard work."

"I will look forward to that Harold. Is there anything I can do for you ?"

"Just take me fishing if I get to Mexico again Leal."

"I will. Please come see us when you can."

"I accept you invitation. Please tell your wife and children hello. I am sending my prayers to all of you."

"Thank you my friend."

After hanging up the phone, Harold reflected on his time in Mexico, the good fortune of finding Luisa again, and their time together. The flood of memories overwhelmed him, and he felt a stream of tears come to his eyes. He was still not over losing Luisa, and hoped that he would never lose his love for her.

Love and Death in the Dominican Republic

After sitting in his chair by the window and looking at his loyal friends, the birds and the squirrels, for a few moments, he went to his bedroom and entered the large walk-in closet. He took down a large box from the white metal racks above the clothes and sat down on the bed. He took the contents out of the box and placed them next to him, on the bed.

He waded through the pile of mementos from he and Luisa's time together in Mexico until he came to a large manila-colored envelope. He then removed the two eight-by-ten-inch pictures he wanted. One picture was of Luisa and the Servidor children at the playground where she had watched them as their nanny.

The second picture was of Luisa and the Servidor family at the Mexico City airport on the day he and she had flown to America to start their new life together. He looked at the faces of the people in the picture. All were smiling broadly. Luisa had her arms around he children, who were also holding her hands.

Gatewood placed the picture and a personal note in the envelope, then looked at Luisa's pictures for the last time before sealing the flap. With tears in his eyes, he said, "Yes, she was very special. I loved her."

Chapter 12

Ready To Sting

September 17

Salvador Masas, known as El Avispon Picante, the "stinging hornet" was hopping mad. He was ready to sting his opponents. He had lost his "cash cow", the consistent flow of drugs from Columbia that he turned into street profits in Mexico and shipped to the United States and Canada for distribution gains.

The United States had learned of the shipping routes, drop points, and shipping schedules of his drug supply through the primary route from Venezuela through Central America, and to his beloved Mexico. He loved Mexico because it was the country of his birth and because he could operate freely in the drug market with the blessings of the government and the military.

Now, he seethed with anger that those fruitful associations had been compromised for a short period of time. Masas was used to getting his own way and the inability to control the flow of his product had gotten his danger up. He was itching to correct the situation and then make the guilty parties for his misery pay the price, in blood.

Masas had always been violent. As a child, he maintained a permanent chip on his shoulder and was quick to address any situation with his fists rather than through negotiation and cooperation.

He had joined the cartel after suffering a poor childhood, where he had always lived one step ahead of total poverty. He had shot through the ranks of the organization due to his intelligence, cunning, skill set, and a total enjoyment of his personal version of ruthless killing.

He had killed unabatedly at all levels of the cartel. Rival cartel members, military personnel, police officers, politicians, tourists, and all levels of citizens were all victims of his bloodlust and desire to become a capo of the cartel. He had become a "made man" in the cartel when he killed a drug pusher who had refused to pony up the cartel's share of the transactions. He had killed his mentor when it became evident that he could seize control of the cartel, located in Northern Mexico.

He had eliminated rival capos when it suited his goal for consolidating power, with himself in control. One-by-one, he had sent friends and enemies to the graveyard in his quest to be the head of the largest, most powerful organization of all the cartels in Mexico. He remained in power by continuing his vise-like grip on the drug trade, working with the politicians, military, and police at all levels, and using an approach that "when cash will not buy you what you need, bullets and murder will".

He was feared by all people in the country, and had become a massive problem for all of the law enforcement agencies in the world. He was on

Hal Graff

America's ten most wanted list, ranking number one. He was well-known to Fermin Zuzen and the Agence de Renseignement, as he was the organization's most popular, desired target, also being number one on their list of criminals.

His operation had enjoyed a good working relationship as a client and smuggler of drugs for the Columbian and Venezuelan cartels and the TCPLM, and had grown as a the preeminent drug trafficking cartel when the United States began cooperating with the above mentioned governments to crack down on the cartels. His business savvy and ruthlessness allowed him to seize the opportunity, and become the most successful, powerful drug cartel in the world.

He developed distribution channels into America. His production facilities and an organization that ran as smooth as a fine, Swiss watch allowed him to become one of the richest people in the world. His organizational members loved him. They also feared him, as they knew they were only one disloyal act away from meeting their maker. They dared not to step out of line. He demanded, and received, total respect and control of the operation from the tinniest detail to the most sophisticated operational plan. He was master of his domain.

He had many homes and safe houses throughout Mexico and other countries, and had avoided numerous attempts by the United States and the Agence de Renseignement to capture, arrest, and extradite him to face prosecution and jail time. He had the resources to pay off the politicians, to prevent extradition if captured, to support his upscale lifestyle, and to maintain his freedom. His inner circle consisted of intelligent, loyal employees and a well-trained, and heavily-armed, band of soldiers willing to die to protect him.

He had socialized freely with Alto Roble, the president of Mexico, and Ramon Nazoa, the president of Venezuela. All three of them shared a total hatred of a common enemy, the United States. Both presidents hated America for its constant interference in the internal affairs in their country. Masas did not believe the story about his friend Roble's suicide. He knew better, as his friend loved life, and the ladies, much too much to commit suicide.

Salvador Masas hated America for its efforts to disrupt his cartel's business. He felt that they had no right to interfere with his drug smuggling. After all, if the American populace wanted to buy drugs, he was only filling a void in the market. If he were put out of business that void would be filled by another supplier. He could not comprehend the message that his disappearance from the drug marketplace would send to the Mexican military.

He had been pleased that new leadership had shown the initiative to keep the military in line and protect his cartel's interests. But, he was also disturbed with the possible ruffled feathers, and potential crackdown on the cartel's production activities. He decided to make a list of the people who would be forced to pay for the inconveniences being thrust upon him.

He had been pleased to learn of the death of Luisa Gaicia. She had fled with her lover, Harold Gatewood, to Gibson City, Illinois. She had met a gruesome experience of torture and death. He did not know who Susana Richards, the killer, was or that she even existed. But, he was thankful she had killed Luisa, as it had saved him the trouble of doing so.

He could not have ever forgiven Luisa for the lost profits, and business worries she had caused his cartel. But, forgiveness was not his long suit anyway. In his entire life the stinging hornet had never forgiven anyone who had caused him pain, as such an action was not in his DNA.

Also on the list was the new president of Mexico, Leal Servidor. Masas hated him simply because he had replaced his friend and fellow carouser Sergio Rojas. That action was more than enough for Masas' hatred, and desire to kill Servidor. The hatred grew and became more intense as Masas viewed him as an imposter in the office.

Servidor's political plans and objectives were dangerous obstacles to the cartel's flow of profits, and the hornet's personal lifestyle. Masas had decided that Servidor would be killed. Only the time had yet to be decided.

Masas had one other person on his list to quickly exterminate, the man he hated most, Harold Gatewood. He held the ballplayer responsible for all of the cartel's problems. If Gatewood had not gone to Venezuela he would not have met and swept Luisa off her feet. She had fallen totally in love with him from the first time she had met him, and accidently thrown her salad on him at the restaurant.

Gatewood's charm had bowled Luisa over and she was in his power immediately. If they had never met she would have stayed at the TCPLM, and would have never given Gatewood the information on the delivery schedules and routes into Mexico and he Dominican Republic.

If she would have never met Gatewood she would have never been held captive, forced to leave Venezuela, and end up as the nanny for the Leal Servidor family in Mexico. She would never have been reunited with Gatewood if he had not gone to Mexico City to scout for baseball players.

Yes, Harold Gatewood was the impetus who set off the chain of events that had led to Sergio Roble's death, Leal Servidor's ascent to the presidency, and the beginning of the problems for the hornet and the cartel.

Truthfully, Masas had hated Gatewood since he had first seen him on Roble's yacht when they were in Cabo San Lucas. He had despised Gatewood's squeaky clean image, his gentlemanly manner that drew beautiful women to him from all over the world, his high character, his sense of humor, and his ability to have kings, presidents, and all classes of people like him.

Masas also knew that Gatewood was everything he was not. People only pretended to like Masas, and he

Hal Graff

knew it. He also knew that due to his looks, lack of personality and manners, and the fact that he was completely devoid of a sense of humor, he would never be Gatewood's equal, even though he ran one of the largest, most powerful cartels in the world. Gatewood was just a ballplayer, and a washed-up one at that.

He held Gatewood responsible for the cartel's losses. Drug shipments had declined forty-five percent, and Masas felt as though he was losing his control of his cartel. He had cobbled together efforts that had increased the cartels earnings in the human trafficking, kidnapping, and extortion areas.

The cartel had also been paid handsomely for helping the United Syrian Freedom fighters, the USFF, establish training camps near the American border. Despite these successes in replacing lost income, Masas felt like a failure, and he blamed Gatewood. There was only one solution to his paranoia.

He must kill Gatewood. He could have one of his sicarios, a hitman, do it, but he wanted to do it himself. He envisioned wrapping his hands around Gatewood's throat and choking the life out of him. He would enjoy watching Gatewood struggle for his breath, turn purple, and then slump lifelessly into death. Yes, Masas knew that killing Gatewood would solve all of his problems.

In Gibson City, Illinois, Harold Gatewood was thinking about the first time he had seen the "stinging hornet" on Alto Roble's yacht in Cabo San Lucas. Harold did not hate anyone but he immediately knew he was willing to make an exception in Masas' case. He

Love and Death in the Dominican Republic leaned back in his chair by the window, and after watching the birds and squirrels, burst out into a loud, deep, horse-laugh as he thought of his junior high school's cheerleader chant. He then said out loud, "The Stinging Hornet, buzz, buzz, buzz, ba buzz, buzz."

Hal Graff

Chapter13

International Law

September 19

GATEWOOD WALKED FROM HIS MAILBOX BY THE ROAD back to his front door. On the way he opened a letter that was adorned with the smell of a woman's perfume. He turned the key in his door lock and walked to his kitchen table.

He sat down and opened the aromatically-induced envelope and glanced at the single sentence typed in the middle of the page. It read:

My darling, please join me in Santo Domingo, in the Dominican Republic.
Love,
Susanna

Gatewood read the letter three times, gathered his thoughts, and placed the single sheet of paper on the kitchen table. The Dominican Republic. What an unusual and, unpleasant, coincidence. I wonder what Susana is up to now.

He sipped his hot chocolate, finished his oatmeal, and headed to the workout building behind the house. He progressed through his stretching, tai chi, taekwon do and Brazilian jiu-jitsu drills and started his transcendental meditation session. He soon realized that his breathing and relaxation exercise was to no avail, as he could not get the letter out of his mind.

He next moved to his hitting drills. As he hit one baseball after another off the batting tee and into the net, he realized that the session was not going to be beneficial as long as he was thinking about Susana Richards. He threw in the towel on the morning workout and headed back to the house.

He grabbed a glass of ice water and headed to the chair by the window in the living room. He looked at his loyal friends, the birds and the squirrels, and picked up three pieces of typing paper and a pen that was on the end table near him.

He thought for several moments about the situation and then reached for his cell phone to make a call to his parents. He discussed the letter with his dad and mom and then outlined his plans for their safety, and his reaction to the "call for a pow wow" with Susana. All three came to a like-minded result.

Gatewood then hung up, and dialed a second number. He was greeted by a pleasant female voice.

"Hello, this is the CIO."

"Hi. May I please speak with Rick Owens ?"

"What is your name Sir ?"

"Harold Gatewood."

"One moment please."

He was then connected to his friend and former employer.

Hal Graff

"Hello Harold. How are you ?"

"Hi Rick. I am doing pretty well."

"What is on your mind this morning Harold ?"

"I received a letter this morning from our friend Susana Richards,"

"What did it say ?"

Harold read the note and asked Rick for his opinion on its contents.

"She could just be baiting you. Or, …."

"Or what Rick ?"

"Or she means what she wrote."

"What are your thoughts?"

"It is too important a possibility to ignore."

Harold then spoke, "I think I should go there. I have made arrangements to have a bodyguard watch my parents while I go to Santo Domingo. I will only be gone a week or two."

"Harold, we have wanted to talk to you about something, and now is as good a time as any to get into it."

"What is it ?"

"Our ability to stop or at least disrupt the flow of drugs from Columbia to the TCPLM in Venezuela and then to the Dominican Republic was working well until recently."

"And…."

"The information Luisa provided us helped us succeed. Now, the TCPLM has made adjustments and are back in business. We are at square one again. They have new routes, schedules, and drop points."

"How does that impact my short trip to the Dominican Republic ?"

"We have wanted you to go there and act as a tourist so that you could find out any new information about the new routes for drug shipments into the United States and Canada. But, we now think that you would need some other type of cover to be effective for us."

"I might have any idea that would solve that problem. Is there anything else that would prevent me from helping you, and also let me search for Susana Richards ?

"No."

"Can I make a call and get back with you later this morning ?"

"Yes."

"I will call you back."

Gatewood hung up and dialed a second number.

"Hello Randle. This is Harold."

"Hi."

"Is the scouting job in the Dominican Republic sill open ?"

"Yes, they called me again yesterday about you."

"Call them back, and try to get them to up their offer. Tell them that I will do it if they can pay a bit more money."

Randle Quinn, Gatewood's agent, called the big league scouting service and then called Harold back in twenty minutes. "Harold they raised their offer and moved you to a newer hotel close to the ballpark. And, you will have security to and from the ballpark."

Hal Graff

Harold listened to the financial terms of the offer, told Quinn he would take it, and that he could be in Santo Domingo in a week. He mentioned that he wanted to go over all of the reports on the players in the league they wanted him to scout before the season started, and to have them please email them to him immediately.

Quinn made the call and then was back on the phone with Harold in a half-hour. "Harold, pack your suntan lotion. You are on your way to the beautiful Dominican Republic."

Harold thanked Quinn, then called Rick Owens, telling him he was hired to scout the Dominican Winter league from October through mid-December.

"That is wonderful Harold. Can you come to D.C. for a one-day briefing before you leave ? You need to know what you are getting yourself into."

"Yes, I can be there by noon your time on the twenty-fifth. Can we meet that afternoon ? I need to arrive in the Dominican Republic on the twenty-sixth."

"Yes, that will work. We will book your ticket and hotel and have a car and one of agents waiting for you at the airport."

"Great."

"We are glad you are joining us again Harold."

"Thanks."

Harold then gathered his thoughts, walked to the kitchen for a refill of ice water, and sat down to outline his options and thoughts about finding and dealing with Susana Richards, if he could find her. He had no idea what to expect, but he knew he should be prepared for anything.

Harold spent the next few days working out, making final arrangements for the bodyguard protection he had arranged for his parents, and reviewing the reports for the prospects he was assigned to follow in the Dominican.

On the twenty-fifth, he arrived in Washington, D. C. After his ride to CIO headquarters in Virginia, he met with Rick Owens and Terry Robbins to discuss his assignment, his contacts, and the potential landmines he might face in his dealings with the drug cartel operatives in the country, and Susana Richards.

September 26

On the twenty-sixth, he was in the air, on his way to Santo Domingo. He had found his aisle seat, number sixteen C, and had settled in comfortably before takeoff when a young woman had him stand up so she would take her seat next to him in sixteen B.

Harold read about the country he was soon to visit, and watched the young woman study legal documents as she sat quietly sat next to him. The only thing he knew about the Dominican Republic was that they had produced many fine baseball players. He read about the country, its history, and its makeup.

The Dominican Republic was one of two countries on the island of Hispaniola, the other being Haiti. It was the second biggest country in the Caribbean, next to Cuba. The population was near twelve million, with one-fourth of it residing in Santo Domingo, its capital. It was discovered by Christopher Columbus while on his way to America.

The country's economy was the largest in the region, with strong growth in the service, agricultural, mining, construction, manufacturing, and tourism industries. Despite the positives, the country had faced unemployment, government corruption, and had endured poor infrastructure conditions.

The climate was ideal, with an average temperature in the high seventies. The country offered many tourism opportunities, with mountains, rivers, flora, and eco adventures, watersports, and year-round golf. The people loved sports such as professional boxing, basketball, volleyball, and taekwondo competitions. And, they were nuts over baseball.

The fishing in the ocean at the Mona Passage where the water from the Caribbean Sea and the Atlantic Ocean met was spectacular for mahi mahi, wahoo, yellowfin tuna, sailfish, and blue and white marlin. Hunting was not practiced. Gatewood had hoped to hunt for iguanas with air guns but both of the species were protected in the country.

Wildlife included over one-hundred-fifty bird species, including beautiful Sisserou parrots, the national bird of the country, and flamingos. Reptiles such as frogs, turtles, lizards, skinks, and snakes inhabited the island.

Love and Death in the Dominican Republic

Beautiful trees, plants and flowers helped make the country an island paradise. The wet season in the Northern coast region was from November through January, and from May to November in the rest of the country.

The Dominicans, called Dominicanos, loved to dance and were masters of the merengue where partners danced close, just the way Gatewood liked it. July was merengue festival time in the country, and the locals lived it up for a month, dancing and drinking to celebrate the power of the dance. Bachata, Latin American music, was a close second in popularity.

Nightclubs galore existed in the capital city, Santo Domingo. A long seafront malecon, like the one Gatewood and Christina Abene had strolled as lovers in Havana, Cuba, was a mainstay of the city.

The city was a bustling mix of old world and new world cultures. Certain areas of town were marked with rows of bohios homes, shacks with thatched roofs, while other areas were dotted with sleek, modern buildings and beautiful homes.

Three major highways lead to and from the capital city to the outer areas of the country. Bus transportation was handled by both private businesses and governmental agencies.

The national currency was the Dominican peso. American and Canadian dollars were most welcomed in the country.

The country enjoyed a strong relationship with America and Puerto Rico. They were also close to

Hal Graff

Cuba, Mexico, South Korea, Spain, and Venezuela, all countries in which Gatewood had been involved in very trying experiences in the last few years.

Negatives for the people were the over thirty year dictatorial rein by a tyrant from the nineteen-thirties to the sixties. The sting of that experience still haunted the country.

The crime rate was brutal with robbery, kidnapping, and drug-related crimes heading the list of actions. Ironically, the murder rate was roughly one-third that of the murder capital of America, Chicago, Illinois.

Gatewood put down his tourist guidebook and closed his eyes for a short nap. He was tired. When he awoke he noticed the woman in the seat next to him still working diligently on her pile of legal papers.

He looked at her purse, which was sitting on the floor by her feet and below the seat in the row in front of her. He noticed an Arizona driver's license. He tried not to be obvious but he failed.

While it sounded impossible to him since he was a fan of beautiful women, he had not noticed that she was gorgeous. She had short blonde hair, wide blue eyes, high cheekbones, and a nice trio of a beautiful mouth, straight teeth, and luscious lips.

She was dressed in a conservative charcoal-gray colored business suit, a white blouse buttoned at the top that hid what Gatewood surmised to be a wonderful build, and a pair of black, one-inch heeled shoes.

She did not wear a wedding ring but had a turquoise-colored ring on the pinkie finger of her left hand.

She looked up and caught him checking her out. She smiled, her eyes twinkled, and she subconsciously licked her lips with her tongue. She then returned to her work.

Gatewood flagged down the flight attendant and asked if he could have a glass of ice water, which was immediately delivered. He then said, "I am sorry Miss. I should have asked you if you wanted anything to drink when I had the flight attendant bring me this water."

She answered. "No thank you. I do not want anything at this time."

Since it was obvious that she was not interested in talking to him at this time, he relaxed in his seat, and did not speak for ten minutes. She suddenly put her papers away in her folder and placed them in her briefcase, which she then placed on the floor next to her purse.

She took off her glasses and looked at Gatewood. A smile crept from the corners of her mouth and she said, "Thank you. That was very kind of you to think of me when your water was delivered by the flight attendant."

Harold smiled and said, "You're welcome. Would you like something to drink now ? You have been working very hard."

"Yes, I would."

Gatewood hit the call button for the flight attendant and asked the woman what she would like to drink.

She replied, "A glass of water would be nice."

Hal Graff

When the flight attendant arrived he ordered a water for his row companion and asked her a question. "What kind of work do you do ?"

"International law."

"Where do you practice ?"

"My firm is in Portland, Maine. I travel. My main clients are in Madrid, Spain, Rome, Italy, Mexico City, Mexico, London, England, and Santo Domingo, in the Dominican Republic."

"Do you live in Portland ?"

"No I live in what is known as the down east part of Maine. The town is called Brunswick."

"Then you live in the same town as the famous Civil War hero, Joshua Chamberlin. Have you gone to his museum ?"

"Yes. I am so surprised that you know that fact."

"If you want to know anything obscure, insignificant and unimportant, I am your man."

She laughed and said, "I like you. You are very funny."

"Where did you go to law school ?"

"The school is called the Southeastern Diablo Law School, in Phoenix, Arizona."

"Phoenix is almost in the middle of the state."

She laughed and said, "Correct. They were confused about their directions when they named the school."

Gatewood then understood the Arizona driver's license. "That is a long way from Maine. How did you get into law school in Arizona ?"

She laughed and said, "I was living in Arizona at the time. I noticed you were looking at a picture of a beautiful lady who was pictured as the screenshot on your computer."

Harold laughed and said, "You are very observant."

She giggled and asked, "Is that your wife ?"

"No."

"A girlfriend ?"

"Yes, she used to be."

"I am sorry you two broke up. You looked like a nice couple."

"Thanks. We didn't breakup. She was murdered."

She touched his hand and held on to it for a long time before speaking. "I am sorry for your loss. Are you alright?"

"Thanks. I am doing better."

"When did it happen ?"

"A few months ago."

"Oh my. How did it happen ?"

"She was shot."

"Did they catch the man who shot her ?"

"She was shot by a woman."

"Did they catch her ?"

"No, not yet."

"I am sorry. Do these questions bother you ?"

"No."

"Do you think you will ever love someone else someday ?"

"I don't know."

"Have you been to Santo Domingo many times ?'

Hal Graff

"Yes, many times."

"Do you give guided tours of the city ?"

"Yes, but only for very special people."

"Would you show me around Santo Domingo ?"

"How long are you going to be here ?"

"I will be there through mid-December."

"Unless I am sent back for an emergency to one of my other client accounts I will be there through the end of the year also."

Gatewood asked, "Where are you staying ?"

"The La Magnifica Torre, the magnificent tower."

Gatewood said, "That is where I am staying also."

They both laughed and continued to talk until the flight was heading to the runway.

Harold said, "Can I call you for a tour ?"

"Of course."

They traded business cards. Her name was Linda Westmorland.

Harold said, "I would have bowed when I gave you the card but I was strapped in the seat for landing."

"I would have curtsied but I was strapped in also."

They landed and bid farewell. When she left she had grabbed Harold's hand, squeezed it tightly, and said, "It was nice to meet Harold. Please call me."

She then leaned in and kissed him gently on the lips, and then walked out of the terminal.

Harold watched her walk away, grabbed his luggage, walked out into the warm Dominican Republic sunshine and said, "I might like the Dominican Republic after all."

Chapter 14

The Barber Shop

September 27

LIGA DE BEISBOL DE LA REPUBLICA DOMINICANA, the Dominican Republic Professional Baseball League, had always had a large following. The increased number of Dominican natives who had ascended to the American major leagues had propelled interest in the sport in the country. Interest had even leap frogged to the level of the presidency of Armando Fuentes. The people of the Dominican Republic were rabid baseball fans, and Harold was going to be in the middle of the excitement of a new season.

Gatewood had settled into his room after arriving, had unpacked, and had reviewed his scouting assignment. The season was not due to start for a week so he would have time to become acquainted with the offerings and customs of Santo Domingo. He had called Linda Westmorland and wished her good night's rest, and then had retired himself. Surprisingly, he slept through the night.

After showering, he ordered a breakfast of oatmeal, strawberries, and hot chocolate, and turned on the television to hear the news. Every channel was Spanish-speaking, and he was forced to try to understand the news by looking at the pictures on the screen and watching the facial expressions of the newscasters. It was a pleasant task as he was attracted to the beautiful young woman who was the morning news announcer. He made a mental note to watch the channel each morning, as it seemed like a perfectly wonderful way to start the day.

He had decided that he would review the highlights of his assignment one more time before he headed out to explore the city and get some exercise.

The Dominican Republic Professional Baseball League played a fifty-game schedule from October through mid-December. The post-season playoffs consisted of four teams that would play a fifteen game round-robin series to determine the two teams that would advance to the next level of play. The two surviving teams would then play a best-of-nine-game series to determine the Dominican National Champion.

The champion would then represent the country in the Caribbean Series with the victorious teams from Mexico, Venezuela, Cuba, and Puerto Rico. Gatewood was familiar with the series, as he been with President Bertalina of Cuba in his presidential box-seat area when an assassination attempt was made on his life.

Harold remembered the incident well, as it had led to him struggling with General Domingo, who had tried to lead a military coup and wrestle control of the Cuban government from Bertalina. Death to a free-lance assassin, Algar Barret, who had been hired by American billionaire Damon Justice to kill President

Bertalina for Cuba's role in the killing of a past American president, had followed by CIO agent Branson Cameron. Cameron then terminated General Domingo.

The league's six teams were located in Santiago, San Pedro de Macoris, La Romana, San Carlos, and two franchises in Santo Domingo. Harold would not have much travel, as he would scout each team as they played in Santo Domingo. His hotel location was excellent, as he was equidistant from each ballpark.

The league was made up of young Dominican players who had the skills that needed to be nurtured through play in the Dominican leagues, current big leaguers who wanted to play Winter ball to keep their skills sharp, and players who were attempting to come back from previous injuries and return to America's big leagues.

Harold giggled when he thought of the irony of his situation. He was scouting players in the latter category that were just like him, trying to make a comeback after an injury.

The league was a respected Winter-option for many players. The quality of play was excellent and there were many potential prospects, some of whom would go on to play in America, and some of whom would stay in the Dominican their whole career and be honored by being elected into the Caribbean Baseball Hall of Fame.

At the top of the prospect list that Harold was assigned to scout was Eldon Nelson, a right-handed pitcher who had compiled seven years as the leading pitcher in the National League. He had won twenty games or more six times, lead the league in strikeouts, earned run average, and had been named the Cy Young winner five times.

He had hurt his arm and was forced leave baseball for a year. He had gone under the knife as the first player to have the newest version of Tommy John surgery. Since his contract had expired, he had found himself unemployed, as no team wanted to risk the amount of money he was demanding, especially since everyone in baseball thought his career was over.

His recovery time had been much shorter than traditional Tommy John surgery. In eight months he was throwing again, four months earlier than traditional surgery. The procedure did not use a full reconstruction of the ulnar collateral ligament (UCL). Instead, it repaired and buttressed the damaged ligament against the bone, which accounted for the faster recovery period.

The jury was still out on the procedure, as it could only be used if the tear in the damaged ligament took place at either end. Traditional Tommy John surgery would take place if the injury happened in the middle of tendon, or if the ligament had suffered excessive wear and tear and was weakened to begin with.

Harold was determined to be valuable because he had been a former player who had endured Tommy John surgery and had initially come back, then had suffered a career-ending relapse. Harold's mindset and attitude toward the misery Nelson was going through, his understanding of the psychological fears Nelson was enduring, and his analytical ability were the main reasons the scouting organization had hired him to come to the Dominican Republic.

Satisfied that he had reviewed his assignment thoroughly, Harold put away his scouting materials and walked toward the door. His cellphone signaled a call, and he answered.

"Hello Harold. This is Linda."

"Hi."

"Did you sleep well last night ?"

"Yes. Did you ?"

"Yes. What are you doing for supper tonight ?"

"I have no plans."

"Will you join me for supper ? It will be my treat."

"Of course. What time ?"

"Seven-thirty."

"That sounds great. I will drive the elevator up and get you."

"Are you a good driver ?"

He laughed and said, "Yes."

"Wonderful. Room 607."

"You made my day Linda."

"I am really looking forward to continuing our conversation Harold."

"You have a deal Linda. See you tonight."

Gatewood then rode the elevator down to the lobby and headed out into the warm Santo Domingo sunshine.

Hal Graff

He had no plans, and did not know in what direction he should head. He let his feet decide and they led him toward the closet of the two ballparks. He had always enjoyed walking and investigating the sights of the cities where her played ball. His first few steps led him past restaurants, department stores, clothing stores, gift shops, doctor's offices, gas stations, and office buildings.

He stopped when he reached a city park. He walked to a bench area where several old men were playing dominoes. He had played as a boy but he had never understood the game. His interest had soon gravitated to checkers and then to Chinese checkers. He took this opportunity to try to learn about the game.

The men explained to him that the game had started in China in the thirteenth century, and had spread to Europe, mainly Italy and Sicily, and the Dominican Republic. In Italy the Sicilian mob used the game as a means of developing strategy.

The game was played with a set of twenty-eight tiles, also called bones or stones. The tiles were square on both ends and contained a different number of dots, also called pips or dobs, numbering one through six. They were twice as long as they were wide and were commonly made of bone, ivory, hardwood, marble, or metal. They were colored white, with black spots.

The game was played by having each player draw seven tiles. A tile could be played on another tile until a player ran out of tiles. The number of points was determined by the number of accumulated pips on the tiles accumulated at the end of the game. The country loved the game and even had a competitive professional league.

After his domino lesson, Harold moved on down the street. He suddenly stopped in his tracks and laughed out loud. He had seen an old-fashioned barber pole, complete with red, white, and blue stripes. His laughter was brought out by the memory from his time in South Korea when he was playing baseball for the Seoul Cranes.

When he first joined the team he had asked where he could get his haircut. His Korean teammates urged him to look for a barber pole, walk into the building, and request all of its services. Little did he know that in South Korea the barber pole symbolized a front for a brothel. He became the butt of the joke for his Korean teammates.

He walked into the barbershop and sat down. He was in the company of seven citizens of Santo Domingo, who were discussing the upcoming baseball season. The shop was complete with three barber chairs, each having adjustable levers to raise the chairs' height. Two of the chairs used a foot pedal to pump the chair higher. A third chair used a hand lever to do the same thing.

Both chairs also rotated in a circle so a customer could be whirled around to see the results of his haircut in the mirror behind the counter. Also, both chairs could be titled backwards so that a customer's hair could be washed or his face could be shaved.

Hal Graff

Both chairs were very old, and were made of metal and leather. They were heavy, offered high seating for the client, and headrests and footrests. Behind the chairs, on the counters, were manual and electric hair clippers, sharp, long-bladed scissors, cloths to used for heating and placing on a customer's face prior to a shave, talcum powder, hairbrushes, paper to place round the customer's neck prior to a shave, combs, and hand mirrors to allow the customer to see the back of his head when his haircut was complete.

Also present were beard softening cream, hair cream, hair spray, tonic, hair wax, shaving oil to soften up a customer's skin before a shave, shaving brushes to apply shaving cream, straight razors, and mustache wax.

The shop was decked out in white. The walls and tiled floors were adorned in white. Circular fans for crating cool air were placed in the ceiling above the barber chairs. Framed pictures of the greatest baseball players, past and present, of the Dominican Republic were hung on the wall.

Gatewood took advantage of the local experts to find out about each player. He listened intently as the seven men, five customers and two barbers, discussed each player's strengths and weaknesses. He was not only amazed by the knowledge the men possessed about the players but he was surprised to learn that they knew about the American teams moving their baseball academies to the Dominican Republic from Venezuela due to the massive problems within the country.

Love and Death in the Dominican Republic

The men were loyal fans and attended most every game. Gatewood decided that they were a good source of information, and that he could pick their brains about prospects when he was unable to scout a game. He would use them like Sherlock Holmes did with his Baker Street Irregulars when they alerted him of events related to a crime he was solving.

Their feedback would also allow him to take Ernie White's advice. White had advised him in Mexico City that he should find himself a nice girlfriend to help pass the time when he was not scouting. The advice was uppermost on his mind, as his thoughts were centered on meeting Linda Westmorland later in the evening. Harold also knew that a barbershop was also a source of information for events happening in the area. He would use his association with the men to help find out information about the drug trade.

Harold thanked his new friends at the barbershop and then headed down the street to see what other adventures might be ahead. He passed more shops, looked at items in a gift shop, and window-shopped for a few blocks. His walk was interrupted by a comment from a heavy-set woman clad in a long white-colored skirt, bright turquoise-blue-colored blouse, and leather sandals. She wore large hooped-shaped earrings that dangled from her ears like anvils.

Harold said to her, "I am sorry Mam. I did not hear what you said."

"I said that I know why you are here."

Gatewood thought, "I'll bite." He then said, "Why am I here ?"

"You are here to find baseball players."

Amazed with what he had heard, he said, "How do you know that ?"

"The spirits told me."

"Mam, it was in the newspaper that I was coming here to do that."

"The spirits do not read the newspaper."

"What spirits ?"

"Dominican Vudu spirits."

"Really ?"

"Yes. They tell me what lies ahead for you."

"What is that ?"

"You face danger from your enemies, old and new."

"How would you help me ?"

"I will call upon Belie Belcan, our patron saint of justice and protection, to watch over your safety."

"Why would you do that ?"

"Because that is my mission in life. I use my religion, vudu, to protect people who will come to believe in its magic."

"What will that cost me ?"

"Nothing. I am in what your religion calls a guardian angel."

"I am not convinced."

"That is what all skeptics say. You will also face danger tonight."

"How will that happen ?"

"It will come from an unexpected direction."

"I thank you for your concern Mam but I am just having supper with a friend tonight."

"Danger lurks my son."

"I thank you for your input Mam. I must return now as I have things to do."

"Yes, return to room one hundred."

"How did you know that ?"

"It is a very easy question to answer."

Gatewood thought, "It is common knowledge that I always ask for room one hundred."

"I will see you again my son. You will be back. Do not be afraid. I will help protect you."

Harold thanked the lady and walked back to his hotel to get ready for his date with Linda Westmorland. After showering, and getting ready for his date, he walked to the elevator and pushed the number six. As he rode up to the sixth floor he thought, "What silliness. I am only meeting Linda. She did not seem dangerous to me."

Chapter 15

607

September 27

HAROLD KNOCKED ON THE DOOR OF room six hundred and seven, and waited for Linda Westmorland to welcome him for their date. He had looked forward all day to their being together. Even while he was strolling the streets, watching the men play dominoes, listening to the locales talk baseball at the barber shop, and talking with the voodoo lady, his thoughts were still on Linda.

She opened the door and smiled. She was dressed in a pale blue dress that stopped at her shoulders, had long earrings that drooped two inches below her ear lobes, and wore a matching light-pale-blue ribbon in her hair. She wore light-blue shoes with one inch heels. Harold's eyes followed her legs up from her shoes and to the bottom of her dress, which stopped two inches above her knees.

He then looked at Linda and said, "Wow ! You look great."

Harold's unexpected shout of approval startled Linda but she soon broke out into laughter as she realized, one, that he did it to make her relax and laugh, and two, he meant it, as she could tell from his smile and his eyes. She threw her arms around Gatewood's neck, hugged him tightly, and whispered in his ear, "That was the nicest, most surprising hello I have ever received. I loved it."

Harold laughed and said, "I meant it. You look spectacular."

She hugged him again. Little did he know that she had dreamed of this moment for a very long time.

Harold said, "Where are you taking me tonight Linda ?"

"I know that you eat light, like salads, don't eat too much meat other than chicken or turkey, and drink lots of water. I know you like to work out, and the results are obvious. So, I thought we would go to a traditional Dominican Republic restaurant and you can order what you like."

"How do you know that about me Linda ?"

"You are a very famous man. You are a baseball player, a business and farm owner, are intelligent, have a doctoral degree, love the outdoors, and like to travel on hunting and fishing trips to beautiful places in the world. I know that you are a Renaissance man Harold Gatewood."

"Thanks for the compliments."

"I am the president of your fan club and I have been doing research on you."

"You flatter me too much."

"I mean it Harold. I liked you from the first minute we met on the plane."

"I liked you also. I was hoping you would be sitting in the empty seat next to me when you were walking down the aisle."

"So was I."

"Well Linda, look how nice it has worked out."

She giggled and said that she agreed. She then suggested they head to the restaurant.

"Should I drive tonight Linda ?"

"No. It is only a short distance. It will be nice to walk, plus we can talk on the way."

They held hands, talked, and laughed on the way to the Club de Cena Dominicana, the Dominicana Supper Club.

Harold asked, "What kind of food is on the menu ?"

"Excepcionial y tradicional cocina Dominicana"

"Exceptional and traditional Dominican cuisine, correct ?"

"Excellent Harold. You speak Spanish very well."

Gatewood laughed and said, "Linda, my high school Spanish teacher would disagree with you."

"Why ?"

"Because after two years of it in high school she told me that she could write all the Spanish I knew on a postage stamp an she would have room left over."

"Oh stop it Harold. No one is that grammatically challenged after two years of classes. What did you tell her after she said that ridiculous comment to you ?"

He laughed and said, "What could I say ? It was true."

They entered and were ushered to their table. They talked for several minutes and were finally ready to order. Linda ordered guisados, which consisted of meat, fish, bell peppers, onion, garlic, celery, and olives, a house salad, and coffee with cream and sugar. Harold followed with moro de guandules, yellow rice with peas, olives and onions. He asked the waitress to substitute chicken for the traditional pork. He also had a house salad, and ice water to drink.

They talked and ate, being careful not to make a mistake of spilling their food or drinks. Linda recounted how one of her girlfriends would always try to make her laugh when they were eating. Harold told the story of one of his friends who had done the same thing. They both agreed that that was what friends were for. Harold asked about her childhood.

Linda said her parents had spilt up when she was young. The family was living in Nebraska at the time. After the divorce Linda moved to Brunswick, Maine where she stayed from age eleven through high school. She then went to college in California, and law school in Arizona, as she had mentioned on the plane.

Harold told her that he had spent all of his school years, kindergarten through high school, in Gibson City. He then went to his undergraduate and master's college years close to his home, and then started playing baseball. He earned a doctorate while he was still playing in the big leagues.

After dinner they danced to slow music at the restaurant, but avoided the fast ones, as Linda was wearing short heels and did not want to sprain her ankle. During the last slow dance Linda whispered in Harold's ear, "I have had fun tonight Harold."

"So have I Linda."

"Harold, I want you to take me back to the hotel now. I want to make love with you all night long."

Harold was surprised by her comment and looked into her eyes. She kissed him passionately, after which Linda honored her promise to take Harold to supper and paid the bill. Harold left the tip and they walked back to the hotel, talking and holding hands.

They rode the elevator up to the sixth floor, turned the key in the lock, shut the door, and kissed their way to the bed. Harold unzipped her dress in the back, and they both laughed as it made a "swoosh" sound as it slid down her body to the floor. They took turns helping each other out of their clothes, and were soon in bed.

They talked for a short time and then made love several times during the night, being interrupted by short naps in between the glorious events.

The next morning Linda was up early, getting ready for work. When it was time to leave she walked to the bed, sat down, and stroked Harold's hair. He responded and said, "Good morning."

She returned the comment, and then said that last night had been the nicest night of her life. Harold said that he had loved being with her and that she was even more wonderful that he had hoped. She said that she needed to go to work and that she would like to see him after supper tonight if he did not have other plans. He said that he did not have any plans and asked her what time was good for her.

"Nine tonight, after I finish work and clean up."

"Do you want to go out ?"

"No, I want to stay in with you. Please come to my room."

"Okay. Do you need a ride to work ?"

"No. My law firm is just down the street, at the intersection of Guillermo and Campos streets, Suite C."

"Okay. I will see you tonight."

Linda turned and started for the door. Harold sat up in bed and lovingly threw his pillow at Linda, softly hitting her in the back. Started, she turned around, saw the pillow on the floor, started to laugh, and ran to the bed, jumped on Harold with the pillow in her hands and started to gently smack him with it. Soon both of them were laughing like school children.

She stopped and kissed him passionately, then said, "I love being with you Harold."

He returned the compliment, and then the kiss, and soon they were embraced in a passionate love-making session once again. After twenty minutes, she said that she had to go to work as she was late. She kissed him gently and said, "We can pick this up again when I see you tonight." She then walked to the door. She stopped, turned around, smiled, and said, "I will see you at nine tonight Harold. Have a fun day." She then blew him a kiss and headed off to work.

He could not wait for her to return from work and be with him in the evening.

Hal Graff

Chapter 16

A Note

October 3

IN THE WEEK THAT GATEWOOD AND LINDA had been together his life in the Dominican Republic had stabilized very nicely. Little did he know that his pleasant lifestyle was about to change.

His daily routine included kissing Linda as she left for her office, completing his workout routine, taking a walk, watching the old men play dominoes, visiting with his friends at the barber shop, and speaking with the voodoo lady to see if she thought he would live through the night. He often laughed about her statement as Linda was wearing him out with nonstop affection. He certainly was not complaining, and the two had grown very close.

Today, right on schedule, he kissed Linda goodbye and headed to the hotel fitness center. He completed his stretching, relaxation and breathing exercises, weight training, and running on the treadmill, and after a shower, took the elevator down to the main lobby. The front desk clerk motioned for him to come to the counter, and said, "Mr. Gatewood, there is a note for you."

Love and Death in the Dominican Republic

He walked out the door, reading as he walked. He stopped in his tracks and reread the note two more times. It stated: "Mr. Gatewood I can be of help to you. I know the drug cartel's schedule of arriving shipments, and the drop locations. I also know their departure schedules and locations. You will be approached by a person who will ask you if you would like to go see a cockfight. You should say yes. He will take you to the location this evening and advise you how we can work together. Come alone."

Harold looked around to see if anyone was watching him. The coast was clear so he decided to follow his regular routine and be aware of anything unusual, good or bad.

His first stop was the park where the domino players were already in full swing. He talked with them and watched them play several games. Nothing out of the usual took place. Thinking that nothing was going to happen at this location he moved ahead to his next stop, the barbershop.

"Hello gentlemen."

A round of helloes from his seven friends greeted his comment.

"What is new at the barbershop today ? Is anyone getting scalped ?" Harold cringed at his last statement as he remembered the fate that had befallen the three executives at the Placer de los Lectores book publishing company.

Hal Graff

"It is the same old thing Harold. We were wondering what you have thought of our baseball players here now that the season has opened."

"There are some good prospects in the league. I am looking forward to scouting them and following their progress. What do you guys think ?"

"Yes, there are some good players here. We like right-handed pitcher everyone hopes can return to his prior greatness."

"You mean Eldon Nelson ?"

"Yes. Did you bat against him when you were playing ?"

"Yes."

"How did you do ?"

Gatewood laughed and said, "I contributed to his strikeout total several times."

"Come on Harold, you didn't strike out every time did you ?"

"No. I actually did fairly well against him."

"Did you hit an homeruns off of him ?"

"Yes. Three. Two on low fastballs, and one on a hanging slider."

"Was he as good as advertised ?"

"He had great stuff when he was on. He was overwhelming, and unhittable at certain times."

"Do you think he can make it back ?"

"I wouldn't bet against him if his arm is sound."

"Would you sign him ?"

"No because I don't have that responsibility. But, I do hope he makes it back. I know how hard that becomes after one is injured."

Gatewood hung around for another thirty minutes. He even went outside for a couple minutes to enjoy the sunshine, and to give anyone a chance to come outside to invite him to a cockfight. No message was delivered.

His next stop on his regular route was the Dominican vudu "guardian angel". He did not even know why he had made the stop other than the fact that he wanted to complete his regular route.

"Hello Mr. Gatewood."

"Hello my guardian angel. What is in store for me, according to your vudu magic ?"

"Harold, do not tease me about serious things. You will be a believer soon."

"You may be right."

"Do you have any questions for me ?"

"Yes. Why do you in the Dominican spell vudu with the letter u, rather than how we do it in America, with the letter o ?"

"We do because we are believers. It is a religion we follow. To you Americans it is something to snicker at, and to enjoy in the movies. It is serious to us, and we spell it the way our ancestors did."

"Thank you for the history lesson. And, with due respect to your beliefs, I now understand. Thank you."

"Harold, do you have any other questions for me ?"

"No. Do you have a question for me my dear lady ?"

Hal Graff

"Yes, I do."

"Please tell me what it is so I can answer it and head back to my hotel. I am tired."

"My good friend, would you like to go to a cockfight this evening ?"

Gatewood was shocked back into reality by the question. This was the contact who had written the letter.

"I can tell you are surprised Mr. Gatewood."

"Please tell me what you meant by your note."

"I meant everything in the note. I can help you deal with the drug shipments in and out of the country. They come from Columbia, through Venezuela, and are housed here until they are flown into the United States and Canada. They have been doing it for years. My fellow worshipers do not like the drug trade as it has been a blotch on our country's culture and reputation for many years."

"How did you know to contact me with this information ?"

"I know you are working for the CIO again Harold. I read it in the vudu cards."

"Are you going to take me there ?"

"No. My sole surviving son will pick you up at your motel at eight-thirty and drive you to the cockfight, which starts at nine-fifteen."

"I will be ready, and in the lobby."

"He will be driving a black, four-door, Russian-made compact car. His name is Manuel. He will point out the people at the cockfight that work for the cartel.

Love and Death in the Dominican Republic
You can take pictures of them tonight, when they are busy watching the fight. Manuel will also tell you about each of them so your CIO can monitor their movements and decide how to use them to help slow down the drug trade through our country."

"Please tell me again why you and your son do this type of work. I know that there is another reason besides your beliefs."

"You are smart for an American Harold. I lost my oldest two sons to the drug trade. One was hooked on cocaine and overdosed. The other was killed when the cartel caught him nosing around one of their drop sites. He was careless and it cost him his life. Do not be careless around the drug cartel Harold."

"I am sorry for the loss of your two sons. I will try to make them pay for what they have done to your family."

"I was hoping you would help us in that area. My family will be most appreciative of your efforts."

"I will be ready when Manuel arrives at the hotel tonight."

"One more thing Harold. Are you being careful ? You know that I told you people want you dead and there is trouble, and death, in your future."

"I understand now. The cartels are a threat to me."

"That is correct. But the cards tell me death could come from three other sources. Please be careful."

"Three sources ?"

"Yes. Be careful."

Hal Graff

Harold thanked his guardian angel and headed to his last stop of the day. He wanted to see Linda at her office. He stopped at the location she mentioned, Suite C, in the office building at the intersection of Guillermo and Campos streets.

It was nearly five o'clock when he arrived at his hotel. He went to his room, and shaken from everything he had learned today, he sat on the bed for ten minutes deciding what he should do. He called room service and ordered supper for he and Linda, and prepared for her arrival.

Linda arrived right on time, and they showered together, talked and ate the supper that had been delivered to the room. While they ate, they talked about their day. Harold did not have to scout a game today and he told her that he had made the rounds at the city park to check out the domino games, and had swung by the barbershop to talk to his seven Dominican baseball experts about the upcoming opening day game.

Harold asked Linda how her day was at the office. Her answer threw up a red flag for Gatewood, as she said that she had worked on a tax case related to a legal claim one of her client companies in Rome had been having difficulty with for over a year. Harold did not reply.

He knew now that his suspicions had been right. There was something mysterious about Linda, as the law firm at the address she had given him had never heard of her, and had denied she worked at the firm. He then told her that he needed to go talk to the manager of one of the Santo Domingo teams about one of his pitchers, Scott Binder, who had been a teammate in Asian baseball.

She moved closer to him and said, "I understand. But since you will be getting home late this evening I want to make sure we make love before you leave." She then laid down on the bed and pulled Gatewood on top of her. They made love passionate love, and then talked until Harold told her he needed to dress and go down to the lobby where he would be picked up and driven to the manager's home.

He kissed her goodbye and rode the elevator downstairs. He waited for ten minutes then saw Manuel pull up in front of the hotel. He walked to the car, hopped in, and they sped off to their destination, the cockfight.

Harold had witnessed cockfights before. In the Dominican Republic, cockfighting was almost as popular as baseball. Manuel briefed Harold on how the cartel had killed his two brothers, one by violence and one by hooking him on drugs.

He explained that the vudu religion opposed the carnage the cartel had brought to the island, and how their members had watched the deliveries and flights out to North America, cataloged the times and locations, and forwarded the information to the CIO. The recent increase in shipments was caused by the cartel changing its routes and eliminating vudu "snitches" like his brothers who had killed.

Manuel asked, "Have you ever lost someone you loved to the cartels?"

Harold thought of Luisa and said, "Yes. I loved a woman who was killed by the cartels."

"Then you know how I feel. I want to kill every cartel member I can."

They finished the forty-five minute drive from Harold's hotel to the barn where the birds would fight. The fighting roosters lived a pampered life, being especially bred to bring out their special fighting traits like aggressiveness, stamina, and strength. Harold remembered a similar discussion with Aitor Lehoi and Gabriel Domeka when Aitor proudly discussed how he had developed a special strain of Iberian fighting bulls for the bullring in San Toro de Lidia.

Before entering the barn Manuel reviewed what Gatewood should do before, during, and after the fights. He told Harold, "Be quiet, listen for helpful information, take pictures without being noticed, and bet on the fights. You will need to bet exactly as I do. Besides getting helpful information, we might win a few pesos tonight."

The appearance of the fighting roosters were as Harold had remembered them, adorned with a large bulbous knot, called a comb, on their heads and a wattle, called a carnacle, hanging from their head or neck. The carnacles reminded Harold of those on the turkey species he had hunted in several places in the world. He had earned the world slam designation of turkey hunting, killing an Eastern in Michigan, a

Love and Death in the Dominican Republic
Merriam in Wyoming, a Rio Grande in Texas, an Osceola in Florida, and a Gould and an Ocellated in Mexico.

Other bird species also displayed carnacles, including pheasants, condors, falcons, vultures, eagles, storks, spoonbills, swans, geese, cuckoos, cockatoos, and the Muscovy duck, which he had seen in Mexico.

The roosters had spurs tied or taped to their legs, and were paired in their contest by weight. Before the contest would start the owners and handlers would bring each bird out, raise it above their head and parade around the circular ring where the birds would fight, called a valla. The purpose served to display the birds, whip the crowd into a frenzy, and increase the betting and the odds on each bird.

The fight usually lasted one round, which lasted five minutes. Injuries or death would take place due to the sharp spurs on the contestants' legs.

Harold was gathering information on the cartel members that he would forward to CIO headquarters in Washington, D. C. He was also having a wonderful time, screaming and yelling for his rooster of choice in each contest. By the time Manuel and he had left they had amassed a fair amount of earnings from their betting skills as the stakes were always high.

When they reached the hotel Harold thanked Manuel for his help and promised he would help bring revenge on the cartel for what they had done to his brothers. He then asked a question, "How will we stay in touch ?"

"Visit my mother each day as you have been. She

will arrange any meeting that is needed, and she will pass along information that will help your efforts. If we will work together closely we should obtain some good results."

After Manuel drove away Harold walked through the lobby to the gift shop, which was about to close. He bought a bouquet of long-stemmed, bright-red roses, and rode the elevator upstairs to room one hundred. He opened the door, walked to Linda, handed her the roses, and said, "I love you."

Her eyes filled with tears and she said, "I love you too Harold. I have always loved you."

Harold thought that her second comment was unusual, but he was convinced that she meant what she had said. They kissed passionately, and moved to the bed, where they made love until the early morning hours.

Chapter 17

Suspicion

October 4

HAROLD WAS VERY CONCERNED ABOUT THE INCONSISTENCES that had been popping up in Linda's comments and actions. He needed to verify her background in order to prevent his doubts from negatively influencing their feelings for each other.

She had obviously lied to him about her office location and her employment. He needed to understand where she went each day when she said she was leaving for the office. Over the years he had faced danger many times, and had been crossed by people who he thought were friendly but had turned out to be disloyal. He cared for Linda but he needed validation that she was not involved in anything that could cause him trouble, as too many people were after his scalp.

Both he and Linda were up early and out the door, she to her "work" and he to meet a team owner in the league. After they kissed goodbye they walked in opposite directions. She strolled to the parking garage, stopping along the way at a drugstore to pick up some personal items. He quickly returned to the hotel and had the valet service bring his car around to the front of the building.

Hal Graff

He drove to her parking garage and parked until she drove out. He stayed a safe distance behind her so he would not be seen, and followed her out of town to the barn that served as her storage facility. He parked behind a tree a few hundred yards behind the building and waited until she returned to her car and drove away. When she was out of sight he drove to the barn, picked the lock on the door, and entered.

He was shocked at what he saw. A collection of computer equipment, firearms, bullet cartridges, a file drawer with financial records, makeup kits, false noses, contact lenses, wigs, fake moles and beauty marks, a file with the names and phone numbers of plastic surgeons, maps, a "weight suit" that could be worn under clothes to add weight to a person, and ten passports were stacked on and around a desk.

He read the passports, which were issued for American, British, French, Italian, and Spanish citizens, were all in different names, and listed with different weights and pictures. Georgia Reynolds, Tina Denver, Jacki Olson, Isidora Rozzilli, Livie Callis, Caro Rano, and Eva Bottcher were some of the false identities.

He sat down in the chair by the desk and said, "Who is Linda Westmorland ? What does she want with me ? Am I in danger from this woman who says she loves me ?"

He sat and thought for a few moments and tried to think of who in the country knew he was here. His public contact had been limited to the hotel employees, people at restaurants, the domino players, the men at the barber shop, the vudu woman and her son Manuel, the baseball people he had talked with, the spectators at the games he had scouted, and Linda. He did not think that anyone he mentioned had a reason to cause him harm.

That left only the strangers who may have seen him at the ballpark, walking on the street, or those who may have read in the newspaper that he was scouting in the country. He had no clue who might be after his head, other than the usual cartel and AIO crowd. He decided to return to the hotel and call Rick Owens at the CIO.

"Hi Mam. This is Harold Gatewood for Rick Owens. Please tell him it is urgent."

"Just a moment Sir."

"Hi Harold."

"What do you have for me today ?"

"Good news. I have a source who is helping me get information about the cartel deliveries into the country down here, and the shipments out of here to North America and Europe."

"Good work. Who is it ?"

"It is a vudu woman and her son."

"How did you find them ?"

"They lost two sons to the cartel. I was getting acclimated to the city and struck up a conversation with the old woman. Each day I worked out and then walked a route close to the hotel. Truthfully, the source just fell into my lap, as they sent me a note requesting contact."

"Is it a good source ?"

Hal Graff

"Yes. I went with the son last night to a cockfight and was able to identify and photograph several cartel workers. I am going to send the file to you when we are done talking."

"Great. We will identify them and follow up. We will want to observe their movements so do not try to apprehend them. We want them to be unaware that we are watching them. This is really good news Harold."

"That's not all of the good news Rick. I won around two hundred dollars on the cockfights."

Both men broke out in laughter.

"Do you have anything else ?"

"Yes. Can you see if you have any information on a Linda Westmorland ? She also may go by Georgia Reynolds, Tina Denver, Jacki Olson, Isidora Rozzilli, Livie Callis, Caro Rana, or Eva Bottcher."

"What is the situation ?"

"She may be a freelance hit-woman."

"I will let you know."

"Thanks."

"Harold, be careful."

"I will."

Chapter 18

Operation Shelf Life

October 7

THE AIO HAD STILL NOT SETTLED THE SCORE for the shame they had endured by not eliminating their American nemesis, Harold Gatewood, and all of their membership was still demanding blood for the loss of their loyal agents who had been killed in the pursuit of Harold's head.

National Commander Ekain Koldo had grown old and discouraged by the failure to successfully remove Gatewood, and his gray hair and the deep, dark bags under his eyes caused by lack of sleep and worry verified his passage into his twilight years.

Koldo's driver sat behind the wheel of the black, four-door luxury car as it pulled into the right lane of the highway, and started the sixty-mile journey through the Northern foothills of Spain. The destination was located twenty-eight miles North of La Murdedur De Surpant, the town known as the "bite of the snake".

The area had not only been infested with snakes, but it had been the hotbed for Basque terrorist activities who had struck the French and Spanish governments in raids of terror in their quest for independence. The tiny town was also the home of several loyal AIO agents who had lost their lives trying to kill Harold Gatewood.

The passenger in the right front seat was the Koldo, the National Commander of the AIO. He was on a mission to inspect the agents who were the finalists for the trip to the Dominican Republic to finally put Harold Gatewood where it belonged, in the ground. Two men both originally from the La Merdedur De Surpant area had been tested and shown excellent skills, courage, temperament, and knowledge of terrorist activities to warrant a final look by Koldo.

They had been tested, mentally and physically, to see if they could pick up the banner of the AIO and become a quality field agent for the terrorist organization's most important mission.

The training program had lasted several months, and the four hopefuls represented the survivors of a group of sixty-three candidates who had started the elimination process. Many had been judged unqualified for this special mission due to physical limitations. Others had been deficient in their lust for killing, and were placed in more placid support positions within the organization. Others had simply decided to quit, deciding the spy business was too rigorous, or too dangerous for their liking. They had left, to enter civilian life.

Koldo would stay at the training camp four days, assessing the final candidates and getting feedback from the trainers who had worked with them for months. He had read their progress reports, but he

Love and Death in the Dominican Republic
wanted to see the finalists in action, and look them in the eye to get a gut feeling on who would be strong enough to deal with Gatewood, as he proved to be a worthy adversary. Koldo had always thought that Harold had been lucky in his escapes from AIO agents.

The National Commander was totally frustrated with the AIO's inability to kill the ballplayer, and desperately wanted this mission to succeed. He had lost much sleep over the situation, as he knew his leadership in the organization hinged on eliminating Gatewood.

The candidates were put through tests involving hand-to-hand combat, rifle and pistol shooting, knife throwing, sword fighting, wrestling, waterboarding and pain tolerance, demolition training, and car bombing techniques. Additional assessments were made on the candidates' abilities in strangulation methods, navigation through an obstacle course while dodging live ammo fire, and tests involving how an agent would deal with potential real-life scenarios.

Koldo was especially interested in how each candidate would fare in the bloodlust killing area and wanted both of the future field agents to be retested while he was there. He knew that Gatewood was now battle-ready and would not hesitate to defend himself, as he had killed before.

At the end of the first day, Koldo had narrowed the search down to two agents, Estevo Peio, whose nickname, "El Ray Del Terror". meant "The Lightning Bolt of Terror", and "Theobaldo Gil", his cousin, whose nickname, the "Liberatdor De Mayha", meant the "The Deliverer of Mayham". Both candidates' skills were excellent, with each candidate having the advantage in several assessment areas. Ultimately, the choice boiled down to the specific plan Koldo had outlined. He spoke to both candidates, one at a time.

"Agent Gil, you are a vastly talented agent, with skills in all areas. You will serve many missions for your fellow-Basque loyalists and prove to be a valuable asset of the AIO for many years to come. I regret to inform you that you have not chosen you for this particular mission. I am always honest with my agents, and I want to tell why you were not chosen."

Koldo continued, "I appreciate the special skills an agent such as you brings to the table in this business. But, for this mission, for this particular target, I was looking for an agent of your skills, and who also possessed a less-revolting physical appearance. You have the skills but you are a disgusting-looking man. That is not a criticism of you."

Koldo continued, "This particular target, Harold Gatewood, is a handsome, charming, exciting man who draws the most beautiful women in the world to him like moths to a light. He also travels in circles of handsome and beautiful people. Our research has shown that agents need to be able to blend in with their surroundings. Your appearance would cause you to stand out like a sore thumb, and draw unneeded attention to your movements. "

Gil replied, "I understand Sir. I am aware I am not a world-class, handsome man, or a male model, and I will not take the choice of my cousin as an act of rebuke for my skills. I understand what you are looking for in terms of this mission, and this target. I will stand ready to serve the AIO anytime you may need my services."

"Thanks you for understanding. I will call upon you in the future. Stay ready and be patient."

"I will Sir."

Next in line was Estevo Peio. He had passed the training obstacles and was now the choice to deal with Gatewood. Koldo called to him to enter the room. "Congratulations Estevo. You are our choice for the mission. Your mastery of the training program requirements was excellent. Your choice was based on your across the board evaluations, and on my belief that you have the killer instinct needed to eliminate a target who has brought shame on the AIO.

Koldo continued, "One other factor in your selection was your strong genetic linkage to the Taino native people of the Dominican Republic. Your great, great, great-grandfather married his first wife, a Taino woman, when he visited the island country."

Peoi spoke, "Yes Sir. He was a seafarer. They married and returned to Spain, settling in La Merdedur De Surpant generations ago."

Peio continued, "I believe you mean Harold Gatewood is my target."

"Yes."

"Sir, I have dreamed of killing him since I heard what he did to us in San Toro de Lidia. My distaste for him has grown over the past few years when he further disgraced the AIO by escaping our net, and helping cause the death of our agents."

"You have an excellent grasp of the past. Now, you are the instrument of revenge for the present."

"I am happy because I think you want me to kill him."

"You are correct. We want you to do that, or not come back alive."

"I will come back Sir, and he will not."

"Excellent Estevo. You will be briefed on the mission this evening, and be on a plane to Santo Domingo, Dominican Republic in the morning."

"It will be my honor Sir."

Koldo wrapped up the details of the trips with the personnel who would help ensure that Estevo Peio had the needed items for the mission, including money, passport, and cover identity as a geneticist specializing in sugar cane development.

Knowing the mission was in good hands, Koldo reclaimed his seat in the front, right passenger seat of the black luxury car. As the car eased out of the training facility he turned to his driver and said, "I have said this before. I really hope that this one may finally get the job done."

Chapter 19

Soldati

November 11

FOUR WEEKS HAD PASSED SINCE GATEWOOD had found Linda's "barn of secrets" in the country outside Santo Domingo. He had paid very close attention to her to see or hear anything else that would give him information about her true identity, occupation, her background, and her plans for him, if she indeed had any.

He had also been scouting the Winter league and had compiled good reports on several young prospects and on Eldon Nelson, the highly successful right-handed pitcher trying to regain his former brilliance. His arm was holding up, and other than one rough inning, he had handcuffed the hitters in the league.

He had also scouted his friend and former teammate in Asia, Scott Binder. Binder had confessed that he considered this attempt his last rodeo if could not get signed to at least a triple-A contract in America. Gatewood was pulling for him but it did not look good. He was a finesse pitcher. When he had his control he was still a good pitcher. When he lost his edge, he got rocked.

Hal Graff

Harold was still being loyal to his workouts and was getting stronger and stronger. He felt good. And, his secret was still intact, as no one knew his comeback plans. He even kept a bat in his room to get in some extra swings before doing what enjoyed most, going to bed with Linda and making love.

She was obviously in love with him and showed it every night with her affection. He loved her too, and despite his concerns, he hoped that he would not be disappointed if she were found to be someone or something she was not.

Ekain Koldo had taken his choice of assassin to eliminate Gatewood, Estevo Peio, "El Rayo del Terror", "The Lightning Bolt of Terror", to the AIO national committee for approval. A unanimous vote of confidence resulted, and Peio had finished the specific training concerning Gatewood, his habits, and details about the Dominican Republic, including language, culture, geography, topography, and urban terrorism skills, all of which were designed to increase the probability that the mission could be successfully completed.

He had been dispatched to Santo Domingo earlier in the week, had settled in, and was in the process of following Gatewood, looking for an opportunity to kill him. Gatewood appeared to be a creature of habit, which would make him an easy target. But, it was not working out that way, as fate had intervened and two opportunities for a killing shot had been dashed.

Love and Death in the Dominican Republic

Gatewood and Manuel had been successful in their disruption techniques in the drug supply sent to the country from Venezuela by the TCPLM. They had concentrated on an approach of letting the drugs into the country and identifying the outgoing shipments, airplanes used in the delivery, shipping routes to America and Canada, and drop zones.

The theory had proven successful as pressure was placed on the receivers of the drugs in North America, rather than on the shipping operation in the Dominican Republic. This approach allowed them to operate freely in the country and let the receiving countries of America and Canada, which had more sophisticated equipment and seizure procedures, choke off the supply.

President Nazoa of Venezuela, despite struggling in his position, was angry over the drug seizures as they hindered him financially and complicated his attempt to remain in office. The TCPLM was angry as the seizures were pounding the bottom line and making it difficult to satisfy their customers, the drug cartels.

Rafael Carmelo, Lino Pascual, and Fabbri Durante were befuddled over the seizures and wanted something done to keep the pipeline of drugs flowing. They again met secretly in Caracas to discuss the matter. Carmelo had pointed out that the problem had once been corrected. He wanted the people responsible identified and punished. Pascual agreed. He wanted the income stream to continue once again as he wanted to please his superior, Mateo Amon, and he wanted to resume the amount of profits he was skimming off that were being earmarked for his takeover of the cartel and the assassination of Amon.

Fabbri Durante was feeling the pressure from his cartel buddies. He had promised a solution to the initial problem, and had gone to Sicily to speak with his brother about sending one of the family soldiers, a soldati, to kill Gatewood and anyone else responsible for the problem. After the meeting, Durante again agreed to go to Palermo to see his brother and arrange for the hit on Gatewood.

On November eleventh, Durante again found himself on the same flight and same route to Palermo. He had sat down in his seat, and was greeted by the same flight attendant. Once difference existed in this second flight, when she greeted him this time she had his favorite drink, a Vanducci single malt whiskey, in her hand. She said, "I remembered Mr. Durante."

"Thank you Mam. You are very efficient."

Durante rested for most of the journey, as he knew what he had to do once he reached Palermo. Once there, he retrieved his suitcase from the baggage carousel, and headed to the exit. He spied his brother's car and walked toward it in a shuffling pace. He was tired from the stress of the drug situation and the journey.

His brother, Celestino, the capofamiglia, motioned for Fabbri, the capo bastone, to join him in the car. Fabbri was met by the car driver, who took his suitcase and placed it in the large, clean, spacious trunk.

Love and Death in the Dominican Republic

Fabbri was once again dismayed at his brother's appearance. He was even more portly since Fabbri's recent visit, now tipping the scale at three-hundred-forty-three pounds. His hair had thinned even more than before, and his waistline had expanded again. He spoke in a gruff voice that was still one of his trademarks. His breathing was still loud, caused by his weight problem.

Fabbri spoke, "Celestino, you need to go on a diet. You are becoming unhealthy. I am concerned about you."

"Thank you for your concerns. No matter what I do, or eat, I am continually gaining weight."

"You need to try something different or you are going to die of a heart attack."

"What can I do ?"

"If you can't control your eating you might try a stomach stapling procedure."

"I won't do that. I am what I am."

"Please consider it. I do not want you to die. And I do not want to move back to Palermo. I left years ago and have built a nice life for myself in Venezuela."

"Try not to worry about me. We have other things to worry about. I appreciate your coming here to put those plans into action."

"Is he here ? Does he agree to carry out the mission as we discussed on my last visit ? The details were laid out but we should finalize them as soon as possible."

"He is waiting for us at the house."

Hal Graff

"Good. Have you brought him up to date on the drug seizures in North America ?"

"Yes, he knows that you think someone in the Dominican Republic is tipping off the CIO, and they are letting the drugs flow into America where they can more easily seize them."

"Do you know who it is ?"

"I do not know for sure, but I believe it is Harold Gatewood. Since he arrived the problem has started up again. He may be working with someone. We have had some employees, local guys, tail Gatewood but they have not turned up anything to connect him to the problem."

"Maybe we should kill him anyway."

"That would be risky. He is too high profile and would cause a stir in the Dominican Republic, as the Americans would come in mass to the island to investigate. It would also be bad publicity for our operation. We need to stay in the shadows."

"You are right."

"But, if we can tie him to the problem, then we can whack him and let it out that he was spying for the CIO. They would look bad, and they would back off and leave us alone for a while."

"We need to put "Il Barbiere" on it. He can make it look like an overdose, or an accident."

"That is what I think also."

"He loves that kind of clandestine work. It gives him a thrill. He is always asking me for an assignment like that."

Fabbri continued, "Then he will get his wish this time."

"He will love that."

The driver pulled the car up to the front door of the residence and the brothers go out, walked to the sitting room, said hello to Boldovino Gioele, and asked him to accompany them to the study to discuss business. The details of the operation were discussed and Gioele agreed to carry out the killing and keep it confidential as required by the omerta, the code of silence. They hugged each other in true Sicilian Cosa Nostra fashion and moved into the dining room to celebrate the coming victory.

The next morning, Fabbri bid his brother goodbye and headed to the airport, his business completed. He boarded the return flight to Santo Domingo, sat down, laid his head back on the headrest, and closed his eyes. He was awakened by a soft, familiar, female voice. "Mr. Durante, here is your Vanducci single malt whiskey."

Chapter 20

"You have company"

November 15

HAROLD's WORKOUTS HAD INTENSIFIED since he had arrived in Santo Domingo. He was feeling great and enjoying himself. He was still cautious about Linda's secrecy but she was still fun to be with, and their relationship seemed to be solid, barring any surprises that might crop up.

Little did he know that evil forces were watching him, looking for an opening to end his earthly existence. He had no idea that he was the prey for the evil parties that were stalking him. Ignorance was bliss for Gatewood, but it did not solve his problem as old enemies, and new ones, had plans for him.

Earlier in the morning he had kissed Linda goodbye as she claimed she was to going to her office for the day. He had trouble biting his tongue and not calling her on the statement but he had decided to let the situation play itself out, as he thought she would eventually tell him the truth about her situation.

He had finished the initial leg of his daily walk, stopping at the park to watch and talk with the domino players in an attempt to pick up any gossip that might lead to relevant information about the drug cartel's actions, when he received a phone call.

"Hello, this is Harold Gatewood. Can I help you ?"

"You certainly can my friend. This is Fermin Zuzen at the Agence de Renseignement."

"Hello Fermin. It has been too long since we spoke."

"You are correct. How have you been ?"

"I am doing much better. I feel good."

"I was thinking about you and wanted to check on your status."

"I am in Santo Domingo, in the Dominican Republic."

"I have been following your movements Harold. I have also spoken with Rick Owens at the CIO."

"What is going on ?"

"We have been following the drug cartels' actions. We may have some information that can help you while you are there."

I would appreciate any information you can give me."

"We have heard there is a rift developing between the Columbian cartels headed by Rafael Carmelo and Lino Pascual and the Durante crime family in Venezuela."

"Does it relate to the seizures of the product in America and Canada that have been taking place in the last month ?"

"Yes. They are at each other's throats about the loss of product. They are starting to feel the pinch in the cash flow area."

"The seizures have been successful. We have been doing quite well in that area."

"The rift between the producers is growing and is very ugly."

"What do you think will happen ?"

"I think that it will turn violent very soon. The backbiting and finger pointing is very bad according to our sources."

"We are ruffling their feathers then."

"Yes. That is why I called you."

"What do you know that I don't ?"

"There is a contract out for you. They are planning to send a hitman, probably associated with the Durante Sicilian Cosa Nostra in Palermo, to kill you."

"Do you know who it might be ?"

"No. They have a stable of despicable characters who can perform that service but we don't know who might be chosen. You can count on him, or her, to be ruthless, efficient, and persistent."

"So who should I be watching for when I go about my day ?"

"I know the value a guy they call "Il Barbiere", the barber. His real name is Baldvino Gioele. He is a big guy, and has a special collection of skills with a straight razor. He peels the victim's skin off in layers. He is a master of torture, and totally sadistic."

"He sounds very charming."

"Just be diligent, and watchful. If they send him the attack may come at any moment, and in any location."

"That doesn't narrow it done much Fermin."

"If I hear anything else I will let you know right away. But, this is serious, deadly serious, Harold. Please be careful."

"I will."

"I don't want anything to happen to you.'

"Neither do I."

"Are you done playing baseball Harold ?"

"That is what the experts tell me."

"You had a great career. I even became a baseball fan after we met in San Toro de Lidia."

"We had quite a time there didn't we ?"

"Yes. We stopped the AIO from bombing the Plaza de Heroes and the locations in the old part of town."

"That would have been a catastrophe."

"Yes, thousands of people would have died. It would have been the most massive terrorist action in history."

"And we took out Zigor Kerbasi, the serial killer and AIO operative."

"What is going on with the AIO ?"

"We had reports that Ekain Koldo had visited the training camp recently. Usually, that spells trouble. They are probably planning a mission, and will select an agent to follow up with actions to make it successful.

"Who are their up and coming operatives ?"

"They have gone on a big recruiting drive to shore up their cadre of operatives. Koldo now says that they have high hopes for two guys in particular. The first guy is called "Libertador de Mayha", "The Deliverer of

Mayham". His name is Theobaldo Gil. He is a mean one."

"Who is the second one ?"

"This guy is even worse. He is called "El Ray del Terror", "The Lighting Bolt of Terror." He uses the name Estevo Peio. But, we can't verify that that is his real name."

"They sound like a real dynamic duo."

"Don't kid yourself Harold. These two guys are extremely dangerous. They may be chasing you soon."

"I hate hearing that because it usually spells trouble for me."

"You are right. The AIO will never give up. Maybe you should stay close to home and leave the work you do to the CIO field agents."

"I probably should. But, I always want to help, and the work is important. I feel like I am contributing to something useful when I do my assignments."

"Maybe you can contribute in another way."

"I hate to admit this but it seems to have gotten into my blood. When I am not doing this, and am just at home doing what I need to for my businesses I feel a little hollow."

"I understand. But, the odds are stacking up against you Harold. You have made many enemies over the last few years."

"I know."

"As your friend, I am worried about you."

"I appreciate that Fermin. We are good friends."

Love and Death in the Dominican Republic

"Yes, we have been through the wars together."

"Are you staying busy at the agency ?"

"Yes, there are always bad guys to chase. We are involved in monitoring many illegal activities. We coordinate police activities all over the world."

"You are always in demand."

"Yes. We address terrorism, war crimes, genocide, organized crime activities, piracy, the drug trade, human trafficking, smuggling, art theft, child pornography, white-collar crime, intellectual property theft, corruption, and money-laundering."

"You would need a very long business card to list all that you do."

Zuzen laughed and said, "You're right about that."

Harold then asked a question, "Can you do me a favor ?"

"Of course."

"Can you check on a few names while I have you on the phone ?"

"Sure."

"This is about a woman, who is using aliases and passports from several countries."

"I understand."

"Do you have anything on a Linda Westmorland ?"

"No, nothing turned up."

"What about a Georgia Reynolds ?"

"Nothing."

"Jacki Olson ?"

"No."

"Isidora Rozzilli, from Italy ?"

Hal Graff

"Nothing."

"Livie Callis from France ?"

"Caro Rana from Spain ?"

"I drew a blank on her."

"Eva Bottcher from Germany."

"Yes, I found her."

"What is her occupation ?"

"She is an attorney, specializing in international law. She is with the firm of Bachert, Buchholz, and Franz. She has routinely traveled over most of Europe. She grew up in Phoenix, Arizona, and attended law school in the state. She moved to Maine as a pre-teenager. She has no terrorist associations. She was placed in our system from our operative in Munich who was killed in the line of duty."

"How was he killed ?"

"He was knifed and tortured."

"How was he tortured ?"

"Mutilated."

"Do you have anything else on her ?"

"No. She dropped off our radar after she left Munich."

"Thanks."

"Do you want me to flag her as a person to be followed ?"

"No. I was looking for someone else."

"Okay Harold. Be careful. You have company in Santo Domingo. If you need anything call me."

"Thanks. I will."

Chapter 21

The Note

November 15

GATEWOOD HUNG UP THE PHONE AND GATHERED HIS THOUGHTS. Fermin Zuzen's information about Linda's prior time, and name, in Munich, Germany was disturbing. It was also illuminating. He knew she had a mysterious past, and it was starting to become clear to him that he had been getting close to a beautiful woman who had something to hide.

He gathered his thoughts and headed to the elevator for a mind-clearing walk. As he headed to the front door, he heard a voice from the front desk area.

""'Mr. Gatewood, Please come here. You have a message."

"I will be right there."

The desk clerk handed the note to Harold, and he read it. He then asked the desk clerk a question. "What time did Linda leave the note at the front desk ?"

"She left it about seven-thirty this morning as she was heading to work."

Harold again started to walk toward the front door. He stopped in his tracks, and reread the message. He

Hal Graff
then sat down in a comfortable green chair and thought. Linda had left.

The note read, "Harold, I love you. We have grown so close over the last few weeks. You are the man with whom I want to spend the rest of my life. I want to have children with you and build a family. I have loved you since I first saw you. You were so kind and polite on the plane. You have always respected me. I have been ordered to go to Rome, Italy by my office to work with a client who has a problem. I do not know how long I will be required to be there. I will be in touch soon."

Harold looked out the window and tried to comprehend the note. He knew that she loved him. He also knew that she was fleeing for some reason. She did not work for a law firm and she did not have to go to Munich, Germany for work reasons. He wondered if she worked for the mob ? He thought not but he was unsure.

He was also inclined to think that she did not work for the cartels. His reasoning was that she was on the run for a personal reason. Perhaps she was fleeing a man who was a past lover, and had threatened to kill her. If she had done something illegal she was running to prevent arrest.

He had no idea what the reason for her flight was, as he did not have the needed information to make a judgement. He did know that one thing was clear, she was gone.

Love and Death in the Dominican Republic

Harold decided to follow through with his plan to take a walk and clear his mind. He headed toward the city park to watch them men play dominoes, and thought about Linda as he walked. His mind was not on his safety, and he was distracted.

He passed a newsstand and picked up the morning newspaper. On the front page, he saw a picture of the attractive television morning newscaster Harold had noticed the first morning he had arisen in Santo Domingo. She was scheduled to do a full report on the status of the Dominican Republic's Winter baseball league's white-hot pennet race.

Harold laughed and thought, "I wonder if she knows anything about baseball." He then looked for news reports about any drug seizures in North America, or any reports of drug cartel activities in the Columbia, Venezuela, and the Dominican Republic. He was not disappointed. A shootout between the Pascual cartel and the Columbian police had caused the death of eight cartel members.

Another report covered a murder of two members of Rafael Carmelo's cartel, reportedly at the hands of the Venezuelan military. Another story discussed the continuing food and medical supply shortage in Venezuela. Gatewood thought, "Yes, things are continuing to break apart for the drug cartels and for the Nazoa government in Venezuela."

He folded the newspaper and placed it in his right hand, and proceeded to head toward the city park, and the domino games he had grown to enjoy. As he passed the end of the newsstand he glanced at a car to his right that was moving slowly down the street. His eyes opened wide as he saw the driver, a Spanish-looking man with olive-colored skin and dark hair pointing a machine gun him.

Harold lurched backward as the tight grouping of ten rounds were fired in an automatic manner from the black-colored machine gun. His quick movement had saved his life for the time being, as the flurry of rounds whizzed past his head and body and found home in the stone-fronted building to his right.

Harold had turned around had run two steps back to the front of the newsstand and sought cover. The driver of the car continued firing backwards toward the newsstand, and Harold, as he drove forward. Bullets riddled the cover pages of the "scandal sheet" periodicals hanging from bar at the top of the magazine rack.

Cartridges also splintered the newspapers, sending white pieces of paper flying through the air like confetti at a ticker-tape parade. The scene reminded him of the World Series celebration and parade in Miami, after his hit had clinched the victory in game seven.

The driver then floored the accelerator and the car sped away, into the maze of city streets that would help the hitman escape.

Harold had dodged another assassination attempt. He was shaken by the unexpected nature of the attack, and cursed his lack of awareness and concentration, which had almost cost him his life. The city police soon appeared at the shooting site and took Harold's statement. He reported the details of the shooting but did not divulge his work for the CIO against the drug cartels in the country as the possible motive for the crime.

After finishing the police interview he asked for a ride back to his motel, which the police made happen. He stayed in his room, being thankful he was still alive, and did not leave his sanctuary until the next morning. He called in the report to the CIO and asked if they had any information or developments on who might be after his head as a trophy. No information was forthcoming. After making sure his door was locked and his pistol was on the nightstand by the bed, he finally managed to sleep.

The next morning, the sixteenth, he awoke after a restless night. He glanced at the clock and saw that it was eleven-thirty. He was amazed as he had tossed and turned all night, reliving the attack at the newsstand. He had finally gone to sleep shortly after daylight had made its appearance. He stretched and then staggered to the shower.

After ordering a breakfast that would serve as lunch, he sat down to his meal and gave thought to why he was working for the CIO. He had nearly been killed many times since he had first been forced to leave baseball and had traveled to Spain for the Festival of San Toro de Lidia.

He laughed and thought that maybe the chant he had recited to the patron saint of the festival had continued to save his life over the years. If so, he would gladly admit to being a believer.

He decided to do his workout in the hotel fitness center. Just in case, he would wear his pistol, as he did not want to tempt fate again.

After returning, he sat down in the chair next to the bed and started to review his notes on the prospects he had scouted and deemed worthy of being evaluated for possible future draft picks. His thought process was interrupted by a phone call.

"Hello, this is Harold Gatewood."

"Is this THE Harold Gatewood ?"

He laughed and said, "Yes it is. Who is calling ?"

"This is Ms. Juliana Callejas. I am the female host of the early morning television show for channel thirty-nine."

"Hello Ms. Callejas. I watch your show every morning. You are very good."

The beautiful young woman was caught off guard by Harold's nice compliment and stammered out a response. "I…I…I am doing a series of reports on the Dominican Professional Baseball League."

"Yes, I have been watching them. You know your baseball."

"Thank you. My father played three years before he was injured."

"What position did he play ?"

"He was a catcher."

"That explains his injuries."

Love and Death in the Dominican Republic

"Mr. Gatewood, would you be willing to do an interview about your scouting job, and your thinking about the league ?"

"Will you be interviewing me ?"

"Yes."

"Then I would love to do the interview."

"Can you be at the ballpark at four o'clock on Tuesday, the twenty-first ?"

"Yes."

"Do you know how to find me ?"

"Ms. Callejas, I have been trying to find that out ever since I arrived in the Dominican Republic."

"Mr. Gatewood, you are making me blush."

Harold laughed and said, "I certainly hope so."

Juliana Callejas laughed loudly and said, "Oh excuse me. I did not mean to laugh that hard."

"Why not Juliana ? It is just you and I talking."

"Well thank you for making me feel comfortable."

"You're welcome. I am very comfortable talking with you too."

"Is there anything you would prefer I not ask you in our interview ?"

"No. You can ask anything you would like."

"You are going to be an easy interview Mr. Gatewood."

"I hope to be so, for you."

"I will meet you on the field, by the first place dugout."

"Okay. You have a date."

"A date ?"

Hal Graff

"Yes, an interview date."

She laughed and said, "I look forward to seeing you on the twenty-first Mr. Gatewood."

"I will be there based on one condition."

Juliana shuddered as she thought she had offended Harold with one of her comments. "What is that ?"

"That you please call me Harold."

"Okay Harold. I will see you on the twenty-first for our interview."

"No, for our date."

Juliana laughed again and teased Harold, "You mean our interview don't you ?"

He said, "Compromise is a good thing. Yes, for our interview."

She laughed and said, "Fine. I will see you then."

After she hung up the phone she smiled and started a search on her computer on one Harold Gatewood, baseball player.

Chapter 22

The Interview

November 21

JULIANA CALLEJAS WAS STANDING NEXT TO the first base home dugout. Her microphone was clutched in her right hand and her ear piece was snuggled securely in her left ear. She was testing the sound quality with her assistant by speaking a sentence, the words of which fled from her mouth through the electronic components of her sound system.

She heard the feedback from her sound man Ed.

"That was perfect Juliana."

"What time is it Ed ?"

"It is three thirty-four. Will he be on time Juliana ?"

She smiled and said, "I know from my research that Gatewood is always early."

"I hope so because we are going to go live at three-fifty-five and I don't want you standing by yourself trying to think of things to say before he arrives."

"I always trust my research Ed. He will be here."

Two minutes later, Harold Gatewood walked through the tunnel leading from the home clubhouse to the home team's dugout. He stopped to talk with the team's manager, and soon both were laughing hysterically. He slapped the manager on the back and

Hal Graff
told the players in the dugout, "Good luck today. Always hustle guys."

Juliana had not taken her eyes off of him since he had appeared in the dugout. Ed's requests for her to make sure the sound quality was still perfect had been ignored. He tried again. "Juliana ? Juliana ? Juliana, are you there ?"

Finally, she responded and said, "What do you want Ed ?"

"What do I want ? Are you in a trance of some kind ? How is the sound quality ?"

"What ?"

"Oh my ! Juliana, how is the sound quality ?"

The beautiful newscaster realized that she had ignored Ed's requests and finally, without taking her eyes off of Gatewood, said that she could hear him very well.

Harold Gatewood looked at her, smiled and walked toward where she was standing. He stopped, looked her in the eyes, stuck out his right hand and said, "Hello Juliana, it is very nice to meet you. I have been looking forward to this since I first saw you on the morning news show. How are you ?"

Juliana's beautiful brown eyes were locked on Gatewood's hazel-green eyes. She smiled and said, "I am fine. It is very nice to meet you also." They continued to speak and after two minutes, she suddenly realized that she was still holding Gatewood's hand.

She giggled nervously as she let go of his hand and continued to talk with Gatewood. She had no idea what she was saying, or if her words were making any sense, but she heard Ed's voice again. "Thirty seconds Juliana." She still was looking at Gatewood when she heard Ed's voice again, "Juliana, say something we are live on the air."

She regained her composure and started the interview. "We are here today with a famous ex-baseball player from America, Mr. Harold Gatewood, who is scouting our Winter baseball leagues for prospects who have the ability to make their dreams a reality, and play big league baseball in America. Welcome Mr. Gatewood."

"Thank you Juliana. Please call me Harold. I am happy and excited to be here."

"How long have you been in our country Harold ?"

"I arrived in late-September, and have been enjoying the beauty of your country ever since."

"You were a professional player in America, correct ?"

"Yes, I played in the big leagues a little over nine years."

"Have you played professionally anywhere else ?"

"Yes. I played three years in Asia."

"Who did you play for Harold ?"

"In Asia, I played for the Tokyo Cardinals, the Beijing Tigers, and the Seoul Cranes. I enjoyed my time there and appreciated the opportunity. The caliber of play was excellent and I played alongside many talented teammates."

Hal Graff

"You used that experience to forge your comeback to American baseball correct ?"

"That is correct Juliana. It was a very good option for me at the time."

"We understand that you have a very unique fan club that includes President Bertalina of Cuba, King Alphonso of Spain, President Guo Gang of China, and President Servidor of Mexico."

"They have all mentioned that they have enjoyed watching me play. Juliana, kings, presidents, and everyday people like you and I all enjoy baseball. I want to add that the people of the Dominican Republic are some of the most knowledge and loving baseball fans I have ever met. It is an honor to be here."

"Have you uncovered any good prospects in our league during your time here ?"

"Oh yes Juliana. The league is very competitive and strong, with many good players who have the tools to make it to our American big leagues."

"How long will you be staying on our country Harold ?"

"My assignment runs through mid-December, unless they decide to extend me through the end of the month for the championship series."

"Harold, what advice do you have for all the boys who have a dream of making professional baseball their career ?"

"Work hard, follow your dreams, never give up, always hustle, shoot for the stars, do your best, and believe in yourself."

"That is excellent advice. Harold Gatewood, thank you very much for being with us today."

"Thank you Juliana."

After the interview ended the couple continued to talk. Harold told her that he had enjoyed the interview, and that she had a new member of her own fan club, one Harold Gatewood.

She blushed and said thank you. He then shook her hand and walked toward the box seats where he would be sitting to scout the game. Her eyes followed his every move until he disappeared out of sight.

She then heard Ed's voice. "That was fabulous Juliana. The magnetism between you two was magical. I especially liked it when you reached out and held his hand for the last half of the interview. Did you two set that up to create interest ?"

"Did you say that I reached out and took his hand, and held it until the interview ended ? Oh my, I am so embarrassed. That was so unprofessional."

"What are you talking about ? It was fantastic. The phone lines are already melting with approving comments from our viewers."

"What did you say Ed ?"

"Never mind, just get over here. I want to show you the video of the interview. Juliana you have outdone yourself today. It was fantastic. This will create so much interest. We need to schedule a follow up interview with Gatewood."

"What did you say Ed ?"

Hal Graff

"Juliana, are you alright ? You sound so disoriented."

"I... I... I am okay."

Juliana Callejas was not the only one who had appreciated the interview. Harold had taken a seat in the box seats and was still looking at her as she stood on the ballfield, microphone in her hand, and earpiece in her ear.

He studied her shape. She was five-foot-five-inches tall, had long dark brown curly hair down to her mid-back, beautiful, big brown eyes, long eyelashes, long slender fingers, high cheekbones, full red lips, white teeth, olive-colored skin, large breasts, flat stomach, a perfect waist-to-hip ratio, a soft, soothing voice, and a smile that wouldn't quit.

Her DNA was a mix of native Taino and Spanish bloodlines. She was an intelligent, articulate, attractive woman who had chosen to work in a competitive career based upon ratings rather than follow the traditional route of child bearing, and taking care of a household. She was even better than he had imagined.

He waited until she had completed her duties with her newscast teammates, and he then waked down to the main entrance of the ballpark. He saw her standing in the hallway as she waited for the news truck to be pulled around to pick her up for the ride back to the studio.

As he walked toward her she saw him and broke out into a wide smile. He approached her and said, "Thanks again for such a nice interview. You asked wonderful questions that were easy to answer. I appreciated your preparation and professionalism."

"You're welcome. We must have done something right because the positive phone calls started coming into the station as soon as we finished."

"That is because of the fine work you did. I was just there to respond what you had set up for me."

"You are too kind."

"Would you like to go to supper with me tonight ?"

"Yes, I would love to do that."

"How about seven-thirty ?"

"That would be wonderful. But, I must be home by midnight or I will turn into a pumpkin."

They both laughed, and he said, "Do you want me to pick you up ?"

"No, I will pick you up as I know the layout of the city better than you."

"Okay. I am at the …"

"I know where you are staying. I will pick you up at seven-thirty."

The television station truck rolled to a stop in front of the building and Juliana smiled and said, "I will see you tonight Mr. Harold Gatewood."

He smiled back, and watched her get into the truck. As it rolled away he smiled and walked back to his seat to scout the ballgame.

Hal Graff

Chapter 23

The Fitness Center

December 7

THEIR DATE HAD GONE MARVELOUSLY and Harold and Juliana had continued their on camera sparks into the evening, and forward for over two-and-one-half weeks. Their chemistry was strong and they were compatible in every way, emotionally, socially, mentally, and sexually. They had spent virtually every spare second of their days in each other's company, and arms.

They talked about their pasts, their hopes for the future, and what was important to them. They walked, read, danced, socialized with her friends, and worked out together at the fitness center in Harold's hotel. His workouts were still progressing at the desired pace, and he was getting stronger and stronger. Juliana often stayed with him at the hotel, and he stayed with her in her apartment when she needed to be at home.

She had finished her day at the news station and had come to his hotel on the day of December seventh. He greeted her with a kiss when she entered the room and soon, as usual, they were in bed making love. After an hour of lovemaking, they decided to work out in the fitness center, shower, and then go out for a relaxing supper.

They slowly walked the short distance from the room to the fitness center, stopping often to kiss. They took a quick swim to cool off and then headed to the workout room. They were alone except for a large, muscular, olive-skinned man who looked like he was the cover boy for a fitness magazine.

He was overly muscular, and as scout Ernie White always said, was "all knotted up with bulky muscles that never worked" for a baseball player. Despite that, Gatewood was thankful he would never have to tangle with the guy.

Harold and Juliana stretched, and walked on the treadmills. She was a good workout partner as she knew that he did not like to talk when he was working out. She had perfected the act of smiling and looking at him while he did his thing. They had a wonderful, peaceful, loving relationship.

Harold moved to the workout bench, adjusted the weights downward as he trained with increased reps with low weight totals. He then laid down on the workout bench, removed the barbell from its resting stand, and started to lift the light weights. Juliana was still walking on the treadmill and neither she, nor Harold, noticed the muscular man walk toward, and take a stance behind Gatewood, as if he were volunteering to spot for Harold while he lifted.

Without warning he pushed the barbell down against Harold's throat in an attempt to crush his windpipe.

Hal Graff

Harold struggled to lift the weights and bar off of his throat. He kicked his feet and used all of his strength to try to lift the bar but the aggressor's strength was too much. He thought he was going to pass out when Juliana suddenly appeared and smashed a five-pound dumbbell against the large man's back, which caused him to release his grip on the barbell.

Harold quickly lifted the bar off of his throat, and tried to stop choking. He gasped for breath, and watched as the aggressor threw Juliana backwards. She crumpled into the corner an hit her head against the wall. She slumped down to the floor and remained motionless.

The attacker rushed Harold, put him in a bear hug and squeezed his ribs tightly. Harold again struggled for his breath but was able to head butt his assailant. As the large man staggered backward Harold did a round-house taekwondo kick to his now-victim's solar plexus. The large man regained his balance once again and viciously unleased a series of blows to Harold's face and head. Harold went down like a ton of bricks.

As the large man moved forward toward, Harold used a sweeping leg kick to knock the giant off balance, causing him to fall to the ground. Harold heard a loud thud as his victim's head crashed against the five-pound dumbbell Juliana had used to pummel the man's back. Knowing he was overmatched in the weight and strength department, Harold quickly moved to the prone man, used a Brazilian Jiu-jitsu move, and locked his leg around the man's neck.

Love and Death in the Dominican Republic

He applied pressure by squeezing his leg against the man's throat. He continued until the man could no longer breathe, and was dead. Exhausted and sore from the beating he had endured, he slumped backward and drew in a deep breath. The man's identity was unknown but Harold suspected it was Estevo Peio, the "El Ray Del Torror", the "Lightning Bolt of Terror".

Juliana moved to Harold's side and asked if he was alright. He said he was sore, but was happy to be alive. She kissed him lightly on the lips and said, "Harold let's go away from here. Is it safe in America ?"

He replied, "Yes, where I live it is very safe."

Chapter 24

Room Service

December 14

ONE WEEK HAD PASSED SINCE THE ATTACK on Harold in the fitness center. Juliana was still shaken as she had never witnessed death in person before the attack. She had asked Harold if that type of thing had happened before. He had replied in the affirmative. She was shocked and upset and asked when it had taken place. He had said it had taken place regularly since he had gone to Spain the first time.

She had wanted to know how many times he had faced death at the hands of others. He explained how the AIO, the Yakuza, and others had sent agent after agent to terminate him. He also covered how he had become involved in fighting terrorism, the drug cartels, and political espionage in Spain, Cuba, Japan, China, North and South Korea, Venezuela, Mexico, and now in the Dominican Republic.

She was shocked and did not know if she could live a life where her future husband would face death on a regular basis. He promised to take her to Gibson City, Illinois, where they would live a quiet, peaceful, enjoyable life. After those assurances she said that she would go with him and start a family.

Once those discussions were out of the way, the couple resumed their wonderful, loving life together. They quickly returned to the quiet lifestyle they both loved. Harold had finished his scouting assignment, and was told his work had been superior.

His employer had been overjoyed with his work, and his insight. He had also obtained more research data from the questionnaires the Dominican Winter League had allowed him to gather from all of the players in the league.

The CIO had been informed of the attack by the AIO operative Estevo Pei, the "Lightning Bolt of Terror", who had suffered a power outage at Gatewood's own hands. Nothing was on the radar screen at the CIO in regards to Gatewood's completion of his assignment. He was free to go home as far as the agency was concerned.

He and Juliana had slept late, showered, and had ordered breakfast from room service. Harold stuck to his usual choices, oatmeal, strawberries, and ice water. Juliana could not break her habit of having the traditional Dominican Republic breakfast of mangu, fried eggs, fried salami, and coffee. The dish was called the "Los Tres Golpes", "the three hits" needed to start the day and prepare one for a fruitful day of accomplishment.

Harold had asked how she could eat that big a breakfast and not feel sluggish, as he preferred to eat light early in the day. She had kissed him and then kidded him that he did not know "the Dominican Republic way", and needed nutrition lessons from her.

A knock on the door was heard, and followed by a voice that stated, "Room Service". Harold was brushing his teeth and asked Juliana to answer the door and sign his name on the bill for the breakfasts and the tip. She yelled to him that she would take care of it and headed to the door. When she opened it a large man clasp his hand over her mouth and despite her resistance, walked her toward the bed.

As he dragged Juliana forward the man's eyes searched for Harold. When the intruder spied Harold brushing his teeth at the sink he threw Juliana on the bed and headed toward his main target. Juliana regained her breath and yelled, "Harold, look out !"

The large man then ran toward Harold, and after covering the distance in record time, brought his huge fist down on his target's right cheek, knocking his victim to the floor. He then punched Harold in the stomach, knocking the wind out of the baseball scout. A follow-up right hand to Harold's chin as he got up sent him to the floor again.

The man then kicked Harold in the ribs as he lay on the floor, causing a sickening sound to escape from the recipient's lungs. Harold was then lifted from the floor and was greeted with another powerful right hand to his now-severely sore jaw. He was ready to pass out when the man threw him across the floor, where he came to rest in front of the room's double windows.

Love and Death in the Dominican Republic

Harold could barely see, but made out a large, fuzzy figure walking slowly toward him. Brandished near the approaching figure's side was a glistening, sharp straight razor, open and ready to be used on Harold's throat by Sicilian hitman Baldovino Gioele, nicknamed "El Barbiere", the "barber". He planned to torture Harold, slicing layers of skin off his face one after another, before cutting his throat from ear to ear.

"El Barbiere" lifted Harold from the floor, stood him up, and laughed. He said, "This will be your last close shave Gatewood". Gatewood heard a slight puncture sound and then became confused as "the barber" dropped his straight razor, and fell to the floor.

Harold knelt down to get a closer look at Gioele. The sight was hideous, as Baldovino's face was frozen in a look of terror. A large, expertly-placed entry wound was present in the middle of the barber's forehead. Panic set in, as Gatewood feared another assassin, perhaps at a window in a room, or, on the roof of the building across his hotel, who was prepared to fire another shot at him, or Juliana.

He called for Juliana to crawl from her current position to a spot beside him, and the bed. They waited fifteen minutes until they were sure no danger remained. They got up and hugged each other tightly. He said, "we are leaving her today honey. We are going to America."

She replied. "I am ready. I love you Harold."

Harold's back was to the window and Juliana was facing him as he held her in his arms. He heard the same light puncture sound and felt the breeze as something zipped past his right shoulder. Another round from a sniper's rifle tore into Juliana's forehead. Her head exploded at the entry point of the cartridge, causing her blood to splatter into Gatewood's face.

Thinking he might be the next target, Harold fell to the floor, and dragged Juliana's body to him, close to the bed. He remained there for several minutes then reached up and pulled the hotel phone to the floor. He called the front desk and told the desk clerk what had happened, and then asked him to send the police to the room. He said he would remain on the floor until the authorities arrived and ushered him out of the room.

Time seemed to stand still as he waited for the police. He dared not move for fear of being shot. Finally, the police arrived, cleared the area, and moved him to the hallway, out of the range of fire. He described the situation to the police and asked that they please be respectful of Juliana's body when it was removed from the room.

He watched as her corpse, encased in a green body bag, was placed on a stretcher and wheeled to an ambulance for its trip to the morgue.

He remained quiet almost all of the way to the hospital where his injuries would be treated. On the way there, he spoke only one time, saying, "It is time to go home."

Chapter 25

"We are perfectly matched"

December 15

THE TRIP HOME WAS A TOTAL BLUR. Gatewood only remembered being picked up at the regional airport by his parents. They had then driven him to their house in Gibson City, where he stayed and slept for four days. He was a zombie, beaten physically and mentally to the point where he was unrecognizable. He was a shadow of his former self.

He did not speak of the attacks in the Dominican Republic. When he was healthy enough to return to his own home, he kissed his parents, drove home, and walked through the front door. He sat down in the chair by the window and looked for his friends, the birds and the squirrels. He was not disappointed as they were going about their usual daily activities. He watched them for an hour without saying a word.

He remained in the chair for two days as it seemed like the thing to do, and it offered him refuge. He left only to eat, shower, and clean up. His mind did not dwell on anything. Instead, he watched the birds and the squirrels.

Hal Graff

His parents dropped by to check on him each day. He smiled, but only talked to them enough to convince them he was doing alright.

His cell phone rang on the seventh day he was back. He looked at the area code of the number of the calling party. He sensed it was important and answered.

"Harold, this is Susana. You also know me as Linda. We spent wonderful weeks together in the Dominican Republic. We are perfectly matched Harold. We are destined to be together. I know that you loved me as Linda. I can be whoever and whatever you want me to be. We can have a wonderful life together."

She continued, "You have figured out that I killed Juliana. She needed to go. She could have never made you as happy as I can, as Linda, or myself. You belong to me Harold Gatewood, and you are never going to get away. You are, and will be, mine forever."

Gatewood listened but did not speak.

Susana said, "I love you Harold. Please love me."

Harold did not answer, and hung up the phone. He knew what he must do.

Printed in Great Britain
by Amazon